Volcano Priestess

By Douglas Weare

ISBN: 1492919950
ISBN-13: 978-1492919957

DEDICATION

For the marvelous Prof. Alice Yang

CONTENTS

1 FEAR OF GHOSTS

"PLEASE tell me a ghost story, Samantha," the little girl cried. Her hair was in small dreadlocks, and she was so tan she almost looked Jamaican. But this was the other side of the world, and Samantha thought it strange Hawaiian parents had an Asian girl with dreads. She was undeniably cute with her small button nose and big pleading eyes, set somewhat far apart.

"Don't listen to Esmeralda," Calypso told Samantha. "She just gets nightmares when she hears those silly stories, anyway."

Samantha giggled. She liked telling Grandma's old stories to Calypso's little sister.

"Once upon a time, there were two keiki fishing in the moonlight. They were on a little peninsula of volcanic rock, jutting out into the ocean. They'd brought a bucket of pitch, and some sticks with wood fiber wrapped around the end as torches. The keiki would make a torch, get it lit, and alternate trying to catch fish in baskets, or spear

1

them if they were large."

She heard quick heavy footsteps coming down the hall, not of the father but big brother Kyle, two years older than Calypso and Samantha, who'd been best friends since they became neighbors when they were little.

"The fishing was slow, it was hard to catch good fish, but they had nabbed three nice jacks, each one a small meal for two people. Orion had moved across the sky, gradually turning above from having the belt point straight down at the ocean to level, indicating it was almost time to go home for bed, and the crescent moon had just dipped below the horizon, leaving it darker."

Jack Fish

Samantha felt Kyle's hand on her shoulder, behind her, and Calypso smiled wryly up back at him from Samantha's side.

"The younger keiki said he was tired, but his older sister said they needed to wait til Orion was flat before they went back. Besides, with the moon down, the torch might attract more fish, or maybe they'd get a different type."

"But they were running low on pitch, so it was taking longer in between torches to get a new stick gummed up with fiber and pitch on the end, and then lit. A cool breeze was on the water, and the waves died down, splashing more silently, ever more silently, against the rocks."

Esmeralda swallowed hard and pulled the blanket up under her chin with both hands.

"Wa-ooooooooooo," Samantha breathed out, long like a strong gust blowing over the outrigger, out in the empty space between the islands. "Though the wind gusted stronger, the waves were eerily silent, and even the sound of the wind was muted, and they felt they were being watched."

Esmeralda pulled the blanket over her head, trembling.

Samantha smiled. It was always more fun as the plot thickened and pandemonium ensued.

"Not from the land, oh no, of course not, if only it was just their father yelling at them to come get in bed, no there was something out there, in the water, in the darkness."

"The breeze died down and they could feel its eyes upon them, feel they were being stalked."

"'Get out of the water,' cried the younger keiki," Samantha said.

"His sister laughed and said there was nothing to worry about, she was only knee-deep, and besides she had a spear. She could stab a barracuda faster than lickety-split, and jump out of the water onto the rocks in a flash. No tiger shark was going to grab her in 24" of water, it's not like she was in the middle of the ocean having fallen out of an outrigger into a cloud of chum."

"But the silence was oppressive, and the fish were gone, all but a couple small Moorish Idols, inedible but pretty. The younger keiki, scared, started gathering their things to leave, when his older sister slipped on a rock and fell. He looked up, alarmed, as she plunged into a shallow pool between some rocks. There were ripples in the water, as something was swimming in toward her."

"'Get out! Get out!' he cried, 'Are you OK?' And older sister with one stroke made it back to the rocks and pulled herself out, the ripples on the dark water already entering the pool from the far side, from the deeper water."

"Sister had scraped her ankle and bruised her hip, and she was limping and bemoaning the bad luck despite no moon, when good luck was instead expected. It was always this way, when the sea ghosts drew near, as if a monstrous beast had drawn near and was waiting to grab them with massive tentacles as big as a house. So, they decided to pack in for the night, hope for better luck on the morrow, and they took their three fish home, vowing to come back with woven shrimp trap baskets in the morning."

Esmeralda breathed a sigh of relief, commenting she was sure they were going to be eaten, while Kyle complained that nobody ever got eaten in Samantha's stories other than the fish. Calypso laughed and said good night to Esmeralda, herding the other teenagers out of Esmeralda's room back toward the living room, undoubtedly to fleece them in a game of Mahjong. The New Year was around the corner, and they were busy preparing dim sum to steam and fry over the coming days.

2 UP THE VOLCANO

The fire sparkled and cracked, an ember jumping over the ring of rocks and landing at Samantha's feet. She knew she should fear the fire, a couple inches to the left and it would've burned the top of her foot, but she felt the cheery orange glow warming her skin against the cool breeze and intermittent sprinkles coming through the dark canopy of trees above her. The fire was dangerous, oh she knew that. The lava had taken her aunt and uncle. She wondered if they even knew what hit them. Maybe it smashed through the roof and killed them in their sleep, that night so many years ago. It was before she was born, so it's not as though the memory traumatized her. She wondered if they heard the lava flow, if they dashed out of their trailer up on the slope to find they were surrounded, screaming in horror as the lava came at them from all sides. Perhaps the poisonous gas got to them before the lava even grew near. Maybe it was a peaceful death, or maybe it was horrible, convulsing bodies writhing in pain, gasping for real air in a cloud of sulfur fumes.

Here the fire was contained, though, controlled, and Sammy felt protected by it, in control of it. A couple heavy drops of rain came off the trees, chilling her shoulder. She shuddered and huddled closer to the fire, drawing her shawl tighter around her back. It was one of those fancy-patterned fabrics from India, with silver thread wound through it so it glittered in the firelight, reflective threads in blue fabric so thin you could see through it.

A low rumble of distant thunder, somewhere on the wetter side of the mountain, made her wonder why she was bothering to wait. Kyle and Calypso were always late. There was no point waiting for them; she'd have to hike to the summit by herself. She felt lonely in the forest. Her mother used to do the hike alone. Her grandmother used to do the hike alone. It was just a stupid tradition, anyway; maybe she should just go home and tell her mother it was too cold. Or go sleep at Kyle and Calypso's house on the couch, and lie to her mother in the morning and say she went to the summit to view the first dawn of spring, the rebirth of the world, the sun rising once again to banish the encroaching darkness threatening to suck all warmth and light out of the islands, out of the world.

"You can't cheat the gods," her grandmother used to say, "You have to placate them to please the people. Cheating at cards is another matter." Grandma always tried to use marked cards to pull one over on you, and then get you to do yard work. She was always digging irrigation ditches, lining them with volcanic stones, and hammering away at rocks to rough out sculptures. She lived way up on the slope, well above where auntie and uncle passed. It was lonely up there, and windy. Sometimes you could actually hear the volcano. She said it was her best friend, rumbling as it speaks to her, yet it's funny she never speaks that way about thunder.

She felt more drops on her brow. She pulled her cellphone out of her cargo-pocket shorts. It was 12:30, they were a half-hour late. She sighed, leaning in further toward the dwindling flames. Picking up a stick, it looked too wet to burn, and she stirred the remaining chunks of a fencepost still burning atop the coals. The wind howled through the canopy above. She glanced up and saw a couple lone moonbeams penetrating the trees higher up the forested slope, somewhere up the trail she needed to take. She wanted to leave, it was too cold sitting still, and she didn't want to go sleep on a couch. She was tired but the mountain was calling, the trail would be beautiful up on the mountain if the clouds broke and the moon came out. She'd been walking the mountain ever since she could remember, though in the beginning she was carried most of the way. There was no way to begin the New Year without hiking the mountain and dancing the dawn.

It would be better with Calypso by her side. Calypso made the dance whole, she was a natural, her grace and the way she moved her arms made even Sammy feel inspired. And Kyle, well, he just made her feel safe. There was nothing to fear on the mountain, just rocks and the occasional spiny plant you needed to avoid in the dark, but his hulking figure provided solace, gave her ballast and made her ready to do whatever needed to be done, be it cramming for some geometry test or making a special lure for her father to use catching Saturday dinner.

She pulled a small plastic bento box out of her backpack, popped it open, and ate a piece of Korean kimbap sushi roll, the beef contrasting nicely with the pickled daikon. The fire cracked heartily, and she wondered if she wasn't supposed to be eating meat before the dawn. She looked up, heartened by more moonlight streaming through the trees, though drops still fell from the branches with each gust that came through.

Her foot felt warm and she looked down, a huge ember was in the crook between her big toe and the next toe, still glowing brightly. Her eyes wide with alarm she shook her foot and it fell off onto the damp ground, going dim as it rolled across the moist surface. She leaned over her foot, surprised it didn't seem to be burnt, rubbing it and finding it wasn't painful, figuring she lucked out and the unlit side had landed on her.

It was 12:40AM. Shoot, when would they show up, her knees were sore from leaning by the fire, and she stood up, stretching, determined to get moving somehow to warm up. Moving around the fire, she wished Kyle was there playing his drums. She wanted to dance with Calypso. Her phone started vibrating, and she read the incoming text message:

"Dad caught us on our way out. Big lecture, too dangerous, Kyle's supposed to take the outrigger out tomorrow at 9. We told him we'd be back in time but he said no, we're too young to be doing this. Sorry, he won't let us go!"

"Argh…" Samantha groaned. Kyle and Calypso were brother and sister, who'd lived across the street from Samantha ever since her mom and dad moved with her down off the mountain, out of grandma's house so dad could be closer to work to reduce the daily commute. Grandma was almost another hour up the winding dirt roads.

She rolled her eyes and pranced around the fire, spinning in a circle after every time she went around, singing,

"Once to divine you,
Again in adulation,
A third time for familiarity,

A fourth to channel power,

Five times makes it all right, all night."

She loved grandma's little chants, it was always fun practicing them around the fire. Mom always joked Sammy was good enough to work as a luau dancer for one of the big hotels, but Sammy hated that whole scene. Like grandma, she didn't want a bunch of haoles staring at her rack while she performed some pseudo-cultural act for their camera-snapping touristy pleasure. If she could be the fire-breather, then maybe that would be worth it, then she'd get some respect, but she'd rather work in the kitchens or maybe get a job as a teacher. She wasn't sure what she wanted to do after high school, maybe she'd be able to get into the university and study something, who knows.

The dance was warming her up, she was happy to be finally getting the ritual started, she had one more chant to do, and another five revolutions around the fire to be ready. If only grandma was here, if only she could still do the walk.

"Happy to dance,

Happy to fly,

The updrafts take me, as high as the sky

Through the forest I run,

Up the ridge to kiss the midnight sun."

The fire was still burning too brightly to leave unattended. It was a wet forest, but she couldn't risk leaving it. She brought the old wooden bucket up from next to the stream, bright moonlight reflecting off the water and making some of the ferns look silver. The fire hissed as she poured the water over it, stirring the coals with a stick.

"I'm sorry to put you out, my friend," she said to it, giggling to herself that it was silly to talk to a fire, but feeling sad she had to put it out and leave, as though she was killing it and moving on, a tiger of the night moving through the forest, stalking her prey.

Her backpack was light, a couple water bottles, a bento box, and not much else, certainly not enough clothing for the wind on the ridge, she thought, striding away from the upper forest campsite, leaving it and her bicycle at the trailhead far behind. As she moved up toward rockier soil, the forest began to thin, more moonbeams illuminated the mist, the ferns, and those eerie flowers that are low to the ground and only bloom at night, so unlike the flowering trees blanketing the isle, making it feel like some sort of wealthy idyllic California paradise.

She turned her head to the side, cracked her neck, stretched her shoulders, finally feeling fully warmed up and stretched out. It was a long trail, and without Calypso to slow her down, there was really no point in just walking. If she was fast, she would have extra time on top of the volcano, enough time to gaze into the glowing cauldron, to feel its primordial power, as though one was looking right into the center of the Earth, harnessing it and making it yours. It was silly, of course, it was always stinky up there, or it was so windy there was no stench but it was frigid.

She had to watch the ground carefully so she wouldn't trip, for the trail was rocky and uneven in the moonlight. She knew the lower trail well, having run it frequently to stay in shape, as well as to get to grandma's house from time to time when the roads were too muddy to drive.

Up, up, up the slope she went, her breath flowing evenly. She thought of this song and that. The trail went over a rise where the rocks were clearly illuminated, a cool volcanic moonscape, so bright compared to the darkness of the stiller forest. Over the bright rise she went, glancing downhill at the lights of the town reflecting off the ocean inlet, glittering, friendly, but alien to the mountain. Those in the town didn't understand. They thought the island was all about the ocean, the surf, the fishing, the flowers, the tourists, the tropics. The ancestors had crossed the mighty ocean, yes that was true, but it was not the ocean where they settled. The ohana was not at home in the ocean. You could transport the Oha from island to island, but they didn't like to take root and grow their baby na's out at sea. Kyle had one on one of his outriggers, he liked to joke he was going to sail away one day, to find new islands, never discovered, to make them his own, living off coconut cream, poi leaves, and fish. She laughed to herself, thinking how difficult it would be for him to give up pineapple cheeseburgers. Happa boys like him would be hard pressed to really live in peace with the earth.

Samantha had learned to garden as a little girl from her grandma, long before they forced her to go to school. She'd managed to avoid preschool, spending all that time gardening instead. She could grow all sorts of stuff, even up on the windy slope, far from the protection of the trees, only a couple African Tulip trees marking the entrance to the yard, their bright orange flowers a reminder that life springs from the volcanic rock, all in good time.

Samantha's mother had no time for such trifles as gardening. She kept the books for one of the hotels in town, counting all their money, being sure they didn't spend too much on cocktail napkins and whatnot. She was a normal modern island girl, she told Samantha, not a throwback to prehistory like grandma, who some of the neighbors said was touched, or slightly crazy, wearing tie-dyed dresses and engaging in subsistence farming like it was the 1960's and she was on a commune.

"*Life in the Woods* ala Walton never goes out of style," grandma would tell Samantha under the haughty gaze of her raven-haired daughter, Samantha's mother Miranda. Miranda would snort in derision, her big red earring loops swaying about, and make comments like, "Paying the rent and the grocery bill never goes out of style, either."

Down in the forest grove, the orange leaves of a Bird of Paradise practically glowed, lit up by a moonbeam in the darkness. Samantha had slowed to a walk since it was too dark to see the footing. She didn't want to twist an ankle or trip and end up falling on top of a bunch of roots bulging up from the earth.

Up and out of the grove she walked, hibiscus trees flowering on either side, back into the moonlight. The trail was steep here, the last rise before the ridge. She glanced at her watch, it was only 1:30, so she was making good time. She'd run the flat part of the ridge when the time came; she couldn't wait to get back on top.

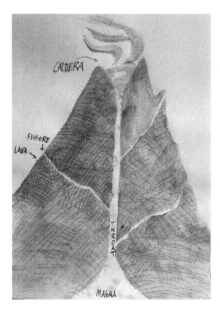

After another half hour or so, she got up onto the ridge, which she'd take all the way up. Far off in the distance on the slope, she could see a single light, marking the end of the dirt road that led to grandma's house. It made her sad that grandma couldn't make the hike anymore, but it was a long way up, and there were many hours to go yet. She kept going, walking at a good clip as the ridge continued up, finally getting more rounded on top, with a wider, flatter trail. Here, she was able to start running again. There was still another 10 miles or so to go and at an easy jog, she'd burn half that distance in an hour. The moon had moved so it was almost directly overhead, and other than some shrubberies the landscape was rather bleak, just a girl running through a rocky landscape under the moonlight, running to great the New Year, and kiss winter goodbye.

Higher up, the trail grew more rugged, and she slowed back to a walk to pick her way through the boulders. The rock was jagged, it would gash your leg quite handily, she'd found that out the hard way several times.

3 DANCE THE DAWN

She breathed harder going up the steep switchbacks that zigzagged up the mountain toward the caldera, the rounded rim of the volcano. The moon was bright overhead, reflecting off the ocean, and it was exhilarating to be so high up the slope, able to see ever further across the ocean. Pausing at a corner of one of the switchbacks, where the moonlight was on the water she could read the wind, parts calm, other parts with ripples indicating a breeze going this way or that. One could see so far over the trees and surf, she wondered if the unevenness on parts of the horizon to the south was actually islands.

Clouds in the distance, Acrylic on canvas (Costa Rica circa 2006)

Trudging upwards, the slope became more moderate as she neared the caldera's edge, and she began to jog again. Soon the trail led her high enough so she was on the top edge of the caldera, gazing across it to the other side, miles away. It was only 4:15, she laughed, she'd come up so quickly, there was plenty of time to go til the sun came up just after 6. Around the edge of the volcano she went, yearning to get a peak down inside. It wasn't steep enough below her yet to see all the way to the bottom, though, but it would be soon. She jogged counterclockwise around the caldera, nearing the steepest drop-offs. She felt her pulse quicken with excitement, it had been too long since she looked upon the volcanic lake in the center, the birthplace of the goddess.

Here the land dropped off more precipitously on both sides, it was not the rounded ridge but a thin rim of volcanic rock, only a few meters across. Going up to the edge, there were benches hewn from the rock, and she leaned on the commemorative sign, illegible in the moonlight, and looked down. The moonlight glimmered off of ripples on the lake, deep, deep down in the throat of the caldera. On the side of the lake, she could see the dull red glow of lava in spots.

What a blast it would be to ride a zip line right down into that puppy, she thought, knowing buddy Kyle would angle to be the first one on the line, no doubt making an excuse he wanted to be sure it was safe for Samantha and Calypso, when the truth was he just wanted the thrill. Guys are so silly, all about action and the moment without a strategic view of things. Not that she didn't adore Kyle, he was the one who'd first taught her to surf back when she was little, she loved him like a brother. Not that she had any brothers proper, it was weird there were no male children borne from her mother or her host of sisters.

Science tells us the XY chromosome of the father decides the child's gender, but in her family it seemed different. Her science teacher had commented that it was the other way around in reptiles, birds, and bugs, with the female's chromosome picking the gender. That seemed more appropriate. If you have to carry the baby around for nine months, your body should pick the gender, not his.

Being on a narrow ridge, it was windier, a strong updraft on the ocean side. She longed to hike down to the lake, but there was no time for such detours, it must've been some 500 feet down, and while her legs were still willing, she felt some soreness in the thighs, some tightness in her calves. Still gazing at the lake, she decided it would be a good time for a quick stretch break, and lowered into downward dog to stretch her hamstrings, and then stood back up and lifted her right foot behind her, grabbing it with her hand in a quadriceps stretch, which was also great for decompressing the knee so she'd be ready to run more. Yes, her legs felt much better now, still sore in the muscle but less taught through the ligaments, less likely to get injured with further running. She'd been cooling down quickly while stretching in the wind, the drafts quickly turning her hot sweat to cold, and it was time to run again, if only to warm up. She looked at the lake again, wondering if she'd ever be brave enough to go down and swim across it. Probably not, it was dangerous down there, they said, poisonous gas or lava could kill you down there in an instant.

She knew grandma had done it. This had been explicitly denied, but in the attic, she found an old picture album in a chest, and there was grandma emerging in a bright pink bikini from a mountain lake, with a smidgeon of snow in the background and volcanic rock all around. Momma insisted grandpa shot the picture on the mainland, high up in the Sierras on the Pacific Crest Trail, but later when she looked on the internet, she found there were no volcanos there. California held no such lake, not with these types of volcanic rock, and besides grandma denied ever having been to the mainland.

Finally she reached the easternmost part of the caldera's edge, which dipped to a lower elevation than the other side and had less wind. Someone had already set up firewood and kindling in the large pit, recessed in the ground. The moon was getting low, and the horizon was showing some blue predawn light, though the sun wouldn't be up for an hour yet. She laughed, there were even flowers strewn about, wilted from the day before. Others would be up to celebrate the dawn of spring later, but she was the lone wolf who'd ring the season in. She hunkered down on her haunches in the lee of the wind, getting a lighter up under the kindling to ignite the paper. She didn't bother lighting the sides, only the center, inside, and she watched as the paper burst into flames, and the kindling started to take light. She wondered if there was too much wood in the fireplace; it felt obscenely gratuitous to have a bonfire when a tiny campfire would do the job. This was a quick fun ritual; she didn't need to leave enough coals to roast a pig overnight. Oh well, they'd lugged the wood up here, maybe it was OK as long as it wasn't too hot to dance around the fire. She pulled a few of the larger pieces off and cast them aside, figuring she could throw them on the coals if need be to extend the life of the fire.

The flames were growing and she extended her hands out, moving them gracefully, weaving them through the air like grandma always did, and still does, even if she just dances around a lone candle in the dining room. Twisting hands, fluttering fingers, they led the dance and her body followed. Something felt odd, though, and she realized she still had her shoes on, important on the volcanic soil but not here, with the fireplace surrounded by ash-colored sand. She skipped around the fire faster, turning, twisting. She was letting the old year let go of her, of the island, of existence, welcoming the approach of a new year as the sun, the giver of life, brightened the horizon. The fire was really blazing now, it was somewhat oppressive when she went by the downwind side, the smoke and heat washing over her, bits of soot in her eye, but she blinked the more rapidly and kept dancing, overjoyed she was here and not slumbering on Calypso's couch. Here, on top of the world, alone, leading the world into the New Year.

"Whatfore you were, whatfore thou shalt be
Heretofore I enforce thee
Heretofore I breathe into thee
The old falls away, burnt and expired,
Upon it we tread and grow
Na from Oha
Poi and ginseng
For all we provide
For all will fall burnt and expired
That we begin the circle anew."

She kicked high, she squatted low, and with her hands high over her head in a spin, felt the first rays of the year on her face from over the horizon, from across space, so far away, yet so immediate and necessary as part of everything. Was the sun not powering the heat of the volcano, were they not similar? No, they were different, the sun was external, the volcano was life, it formed the island, without it they'd sink into the sea. Her hands twisting through the air, she reflected that the volcano was life, it and not the sea provided their principal sources of sustenance, there could be no life on the sea, not permanent life, it was void and as empty as the space above her, whose few remaining stars were fading as the darkness became light, wispy clouds scattered about lighting up red and salmon, lightening to light pink and yellow-orange as the mighty sun breached the horizon.

The fire crackled and flared, it was too big, too big to sit next to, but was perfect for the dance, she kept turning so it wouldn't be too hot on her legs, the breeze growing with the sunlight, even as the sun warmed her skin. This would be her year, she felt somehow, and though on the other hand it really just seemed another day, any old day, the brightness of the sun filled her with optimism. Again she chanted, dancing in time, feeling at one with the fire, the volcano, and the sun rising over the ocean's cold dead void. Finally the dance was done. Her only regret was not having Calypso and Kyle with her to ring in this New Year, how spectacular it seemed, this first morning, the whole year before her, endless possibilities.

She pulled her shoes back on, knowing she should douse the fire but not willing to dampen its mutual enthusiasm for the new day. Samantha strode a few steps back to take another peak down in to the caldera. There was some mist down there, and from this angle she could only see the far edge of the lake, and she swore she'd at least dip her toes in that water before the next spring came, when again she'd welcome the New Year up on this mountaintop.

Her hair wafted in the breeze as she took a final draught of water before sprinkling the last of it around the edges of the fireplace, the rocks so hot it evaporated to steam in front of her eyes, a worthy offering for a worthy fire to the volcano goddess. Beginning her descent, she wondered if Calypso would whip her up some banana pancakes to recharge her legs. Oops, she giggled to herself, somehow she'd forgotten about all the dim sum, she'd feast better than just pancakes this morn.

☐

4 DARK FORCES

Back at Calypso's, party preparations were in full swing. Father had dragged Kyle out of bed to hit the water in an outrigger, though whether for long-distance paddling practice or fishing was anyone's guess, while Calypso and Esmeralda busily stuffed dumplings with shrimp and pork, putting them on a banana leaf for their mother to steam.

"The boys will be back around 10," she commented, "Calypso, can you be sure to soak some kelp leaves and shitake mushrooms? Be sure to dump some mirin, sugar, and soy in the water so they taste good. Throw ginger and lemongrass in afterwards, and keep the sauce around, we can brine any fish they bring back in it for the

BBQ."

"Sure mom," Calypso said, wondering which relatives would come and whether they'd behave. Uncle Jimmy had a penchant for eating all the teriyaki, and Aunt Laoha would viciously criticize him without end if she didn't get any. Calypso had tried ringing Samantha a few times, only to get no response. It didn't worry her much, Sam up on the mountain alone. If it was anyone else she'd worry, but Sam had grown up there, like the whole mountain was her backyard. It didn't make sense, but Samantha's grandma had lived up there through several eruptions with nary a scratch. She had a feeling that it could even blow up, and somehow Samantha would be OK, over on a ridge untouched, as though she'd know where the lava was going to come and be able to avoid it.

But then, even though the family tended to live up on the mountain, not all of them survived it. She shuddered. They could all be wiped out at any time. Mahalo, Pele, we won't mess with your blue caterpillars, and please don't send any lava flows through our house. We don't need them, no need at all, we got enough heat for BBQ, enough heat for pizza, we don't need any 1000° lava crimping our style, destroying Kyle's precious surfboards or worse, papa's racing outrigger in the garage.

After a while the guests started arriving, and soon Calypso was less food prep assistant then meter, greeter, and volunteer manager.

Uncle Jimmy showed up and she put him to work assembling the ping pong table out in the backyard under the coconut trees. She got Cousin Veronica to start frying taro patties with Chinese sausage in them and spring rolls, and she had Esmeralda prep the eggplant to be roasted with pork and Chinese black bean sauce in the oven. Grandma Susie brewed the tea, setting a samovar on one table to keep hot water readily available like she was a Russian instead of a typical Polynesian mix of different Asian ethnicities. Meanwhile a bunch of the kids were playing on the rope swing over the stream running through the backyard.

"Where's Sam?" a voice demanded behind her, and Calypso turned to find Kyle had appeared. Wow, it was already 9:45.

"Haven't heard from her yet, she's not been picking up," Calypso responded, seeing Kyle's face darken. "But the party doesn't start til 10, maybe she stopped off at her grandma's for a nap on the way back, or crashed up on the summit under a blanket."

"That's exactly what I'm worried about," he retorted, "She's never been up there all night alone."

Calypso stopped, thinking, wondering if that was true. Hmmm, he was probably right, he wasn't the loosey-goosey "hang loose" surfer bro guy who'd have the facts wrong. No, he was friendly, but dead serious about some things, and wasn't prone to jumping to conclusions or getting facts mixed up. She sighed, thinking she'd have a lot harder time getting into the university than Sam and Kyle, for while Kyle kept all the facts straight, she tended to get nervous on tests and later wonder how she could've made so many dumb mistakes.

"Well, get your booty across the street and see if she's home? Maybe she's been back for hours."

"I checked, her bike isn't there, her bedroom window's open, she's not there."

It was then they heard the familiar metallic screech of Samantha's bicycle brakes outside. The brakes barely worked, there were no rubber pads left on them to speak of, it was crazy that she was riding that thing up and down the mountain every day, Calypso thought. She opened her mouth to speak, but Kyle was already outside, the screen door slamming behind him. Calypso sometimes felt a pang of jealousy, that her brother was so keen on her friend, after all, Sam was her friend, Kyle had his own friends, he'd used to like to play with Sam from time to time but now in high school, he kept acting weird about her, trying to protect her from dangers that didn't exist, acting odd if some other guy was hanging around Sam, stuff like that.

Her hands were gooey with won ton stuffing, so she wasn't about to dash outside. She'd get an update, all in good time. She kept stuffing wontons, and she heard Sam approaching, exchanging greetings with a score of relatives while trying to get through the yard into the kitchen. Somebody fired up a boom box, the reggae beat drowning out all the conversations outside, both human and all the tropical birds singing to each other. She was glad she wasn't living on Maui, too many noisy roosters there, their incessant crowing was insufferable. She didn't understand why they didn't just eat them all; it's not like they are the state bird.

"Yo, Cal!" Samantha shouted as she entered the kitchen, "You missed an awesome sunrise!"

Calypso turned to take her in, wondering what she'd look like. Actually, Samantha looked better than expected, only mud splattered ankles and some rings under her eyes hinting at her nocturnal activities. Calypso cleaned off her hands, putting the wontons in the fridge for auntie to fry later, and gave Sam a hug. Off to the samovar they went for hot water and tea, and soon they were recharging on dim sum with Kyle, who must've had a second and third stomach he consumed so much. Dad hauled him away to help get the fish out of the truck and onto a cleaning table, while cats prowled hungrily, knowing fish gut handout paradise was moments away.

Clouds were gathering quickly, though, and soon a sprinkling of rain was strengthening into a shower. Those outside not tending the BBQ crowded inside as the rain intensified, pelting down with an abnormal intensity, as though the seasons were trying to get one last blast of winter in before the spring.

By the time noon rolled around, the stream was overflowing its banks, the house was packed, one room full of people watching a football game and yelling rowdily, the other rooms seemingly divided into different demographic categories as some of the older ladies took over the kitchen, and some of the kids braved the rain to set up coconut races in the stream.

The wind was picking up, which was quite unusual for early spring. Gusts were coming through the trees, stronger and stronger like it was the late summer-fall typhoon season, and the football game was interrupted with high surf and wind advisories. Eventually some of the mothers corralled the kids, making them come inside. Uncle Jimmy, undeterred, laughed off the weather and kept dashing out to mind the barbeque in between football plays, exclaiming "What'd I miss, what'd I miss?!?!" every time he returned in, dripping all over the foyer before reclaiming his damp spot on the couch.

"I'm glad Kyle isn't out there in outrigger right now," Sam commented to Calypso. The rain was really coming down. The yard looked like a swamp it was so wet, and when a gust came through it pelted the windows like a fire hose.

Jimmy finally started bringing in the BBQ, including some line-caught Marlin from Kyle's dad. Cousin Meilin put out a big California roll casserole, where you put a scoop of the layered crab, avocado, and rice on your plate and then pick them up with pieces of seaweed rather than have it all prerolled. Kyle was digging into the bulgogi & kimchee dumplings, passing them over to Calypso and Samantha as they squeezed in next to him at a long table packed with people.

Calypso loved the fiery Korean food, but Samantha wouldn't mess with it.

"You know that stuff just makes you fart kimchee fumes!" she chided Calypso. "The bulgogi's too fatty, the aunties don't trim it enough."

"That's why you need to eat it!" Calypso retorted, "Kyle's gonna smell to high heaven, it we eat it too, we won't notice his stench. Besides, you could use the calories after running the mountain."

She was right, Samantha felt worn out, but it wasn't a hungry worn out, it was a satisfied worn out. Her calves and legs were sore, yes, they were really sore, so were other parts, but it was a good holy sore, the sore you get from a workout that builds your athletic ability. She felt her body healing from the workout, but somehow she felt putting a fire in her belly wouldn't be a good idea, and she stuck with the Mahi Mahi and California roll stuff. The gusts were unrelenting, buffeting the house, and she was wishing grandma had come down off the volcano for the party.

Suddenly there was a huge gust, so the whole house shook, followed by a tremendous creaking sound in the yard, and then a crash outside. Car alarms were going off and there were shouts from one of the living rooms, where windows had been shattered by several large palm fronds, knocked through the window by a falling tree. Rain and wind poured through the window.

Calypso looked amused, she feared no storm, while Kyle jumped up to help his dad, Uncle Jimmy, and the other guys survey the damage. Before long they were drilling and screwing a sheet of corrugated metal over the broken window. Some of the guests were departing, though, going home to ride out the remainder of the storm.

Samantha went outside to survey the damage with Calypso, though, and found the sky troubling. The clouds were arranged in long streaks, not at all like those one expected in a storm, but the wind howled with unprecedented strength nonetheless, heedless of the clouds.

Something was wrong. Samantha knew in her bones, something was wrong. Drills were whirring and the guys were admiring their quick handiwork, using duct tape around the top as temporary waterproofing so water wouldn't leak in around the iron sheet. No, there was something wrong with the wind. It sounded angry, blasting through the trees, and the yard was a mess, with palm fronds everywhere, like a really bad September tropical storm or typhoon. These usually strike out further West in the Pacific, and there was something deeply unsettling about having one occur in spring.

She told Calypso she was going to go home to call and check on grandma in case there was flooding or mudslides on the mountain, and she left the shelter of the eaves and walked out into the street, looking up at the mountain. There were low level clouds and mist drifting about, and she couldn't see through them all the way up the slope. She saw a flash of lighting on the summit, and heard the dull rumble of thunder.

Lighting shouldn't be striking the summit in March; it was almost as though the sky was attacking the volcano, the holy volcano. Had she not done the rite correctly, could this be a result of an improper dance to welcome the spring dawn? No, that's just crazy, she thought to herself, she'd just had too little sleep and spent too much time personifying the volcano with the ancient rites. There was no Pele, the sky and volcano were not sentient objects, she shouldn't take grandma's stories and traditions to heart like this. The street looked like it was turning into a river, water flowing across it about a half inch deep. This was just a squall, no big deal, right?

She called, but grandma's phone just rang and rang. Fear started to grip her stomach. Grandma never left the house in a storm, so why wasn't she picking up? But maybe the lines were down? Momma came in, having followed her back from the party.

"Mom, grandma's not picking up!"

Miranda looked mildly concerned, commenting, "Sure, of course not, with all those gusts some of the lines are down. It's not like she never loses service up there, remember how often the lights or power would go out when we lived up there?"

Her mother embraced her, lightly tousling her wet hair.

"Sweetie, you're just worried since you were out all night. You're just exhausted. Don't worry, she'll be fine, you can go see her tomorrow."

"How about now? I could ride my bike up there?"

Her mother chortled before turning her down, commenting how there was too much rain, she was too tired, and she had no business trying to bike up a mountain she'd only just descended. Soon, she found herself back at Calypso's, sitting with her and Kyle on the couch trying to watch some old movie, but she fell asleep.

5 EDUCATION IS GOOD

In the morning, grandma still wasn't picking up her phone. Samantha resolved to ride her bike up there. Her mother would hear none of that, though, saying she'd drive her up. Miranda knew her mother would be quite pleased Samantha had taken her ancient rituals so seriously. It was still a bone of contention that Miranda had spurned the dances and the chants. The truth is, she just felt awkward the moment she tried to do any of that kind of thing in front of people. As with Samantha, she'd learned the chants from early childhood, but unlike Samantha, she'd never felt at home doing them in front of a crowd. It was just way too embarrassing, and she was always fretting about her foot placement in the dance, it didn't seem like she could stay in time with the drums, and match the chant with the dance. Then there was the time she tripped and practically fell into a fire pit, charring her hand on the hot rocks.

She sighed. Samantha was so like her in so many ways, slightly reclusive, not a big social butterfly, yet also like her mom, willing to lead a group in a chant, happy to go skipping around the fire, hands winding like snakes in the dim light during the invocation. How was it that Sam danced with such graceful form, all the while chanting or singing so loudly? Miranda couldn't remember all the lines of the dumb chants, anyway, especially while trying to dance. How was it that her daughter was so perfect, while she just fell into the fire?

It didn't matter. Sam was confident, she'd done well on her PSAT's, one day she'd go on to the university, and all this would be a happy memory. If she tried to major in archeology or ancient spirituality, then they'd have to have a talk about what was practical and could pay the bills, and what was left for myth and legend, or twisted into dances for tourist revenue. She knew Sam would never go work at a luau like Cousin Rhonda, dancing around with coconut shells as a bikini-top and a big straw skirt. Rhonda was never the smartest of the cousins, but you'd think she'd recognize wait staff got paid better tips than luau dancers. Why she still dreamed she'd be recruited to work in Hollywood movies from a luau dance crew was anybody's guess. We all dream in order that we have hope, we all need hope since without it life is unbearable.

She found Sam and Calypso in the kitchen making Denver omelets. The big empty plate on the table near the half-finished OJ let her know her husband Kenji had already eaten breakfast and left the house. He was always an early riser, but he hated OJ unless it was thoroughly diluted with mango juice. Sam was always trying to get him to have more fruit and less meat, and no doubt her Denver omelets were heavy on the bell peppers and onions, but rather light on the ham. Kids these days, she thought to herself, always following the culinary fashion du jour.

She tried to get them out of the house but they made her have a small omelet first. They knew well she preferred to skip breakfast and have heavy loco moco or KFC for lunch. She preferred to get up and get work done rather than putz about in the kitchen making breakfast and drinking coffee like her and Kenji. It was their father-daughter bonding time.

Finally she consumed enough so the girls deigned to depart, and they piled in the car and headed over the winding roads to grandma's house. It wasn't that far away on the map, but the way the roads were it took quite some time to get there. First you had to go down the mountain most of the way to the village, and then you had to take another road up, and then after a long while you took a dirt road back toward where they lived, but on a higher ridge, and finally you turned up a driveway about two miles long that took you to grandma's house. There used to be another small dwelling in the area, but its residents had moved out some 20 years before.

Up at grandma's nothing seemed out of sorts when they arrived. The place was messy like everywhere else from the winds the previous day, now long gone under the warm sunlight, leaving behind but scattered leaves and the ubiquitous palm fronds, heavy enough to cause some minor damage if you were unlucky enough to be hit by one. Uncle Jimmy said he'd been hit by at least ten as sure as he'd been hit by more than one, and joked the lucky thirteenth would likely kill him. One of his ears bore lumpy scar tissue.

They fanned out looking for her, momma going inside while Calypso and Samantha went into the garden. They didn't see her at first, til they heard some grunting sounds coming from inside a small thicket. Sure enough, grandma was in there, hacking away at the rocky soil with a trowel and a hoe, making a new bed in the garden, with the thicket as a wind break.

"Oh, Samantha and Calypso, it's great to see you! Would you give me a hand, it's plenty rocky over here. With all the rain yesterday, this seemed a great time to get at these rocks while the soil's all loosened up."

She had mud splattered all over her forearms and legs, and was wearing a faded red Hilo Loco Moco! T-shirt and biking shorts. Calypso left to tell Miranda they'd found grandma, while Sam grabbed a hoe to help out.

"Grandma, I was worried about you, that storm was strong," Samantha led off.

Grandma snorted. "Don't worry little one, it's not the first storm I've been through. I hear you danced the dawn up top. I'm sorry I couldn't be there with you. Your mother never did it by herself. It would've been special to witness it."

"Oh, yeah, it was fun. I mean, it was a smidgeon chilly, there was some rain on the way up, but it cleared up and was a beautiful night," Samantha said. "But I was kinda freaked out by the storm yesterday, the clouds looked all weird and it didn't seem natural."

Her grandmother paused and put down her trowel, eyeballing her in a funny way, sitting there quietly on her haunches.

Samantha looked back at her, wondering about the sudden silence from one who was usually so talkative.

Her grandma finally cleared her throat. "Not natural, you say? What makes you say that?"

"Well, the clouds were arranged in ridges, not like the fall storms, and you know we never get wind like that," Samantha said, feeling relieved to tell someone about this since Calypso just discounted it as a freak squall.

"I even saw lightning striking the caldera up top, a lot of it, blasting at it again and again, it was weird."

"Uh-huh," said grandma, still looking at her.

"I mean, like I said, it didn't look natural. Sure, lighting hits the summit once, I've seen that, but this was like 10 times, and it only hit the top. It was like out of a video game, like Zeus or some sorcerer was pounding the mountain with lightning bolts."

"Yes, child," grandma breathed out, her face relaxing, "That's exactly what it looks like, doesn't it? Maybe it wasn't a freak storm at all. You know nature works in mysterious ways, cause and effect are all around us, working in ways we can't see. But sometimes you can sense that which you can't see. Don't be afraid of these feelings."

Sam was puzzled. Was grandma going to go off into some mystic silliness again?

"Look, I know you're skeptical, it's only natural. I was, too, at first. But the others can't see or sense this stuff. They can't do the dance; they can't do the evocation correctly." Grandma paused.

"But you can chant the evocation. You can dance the ritual perfectly, better even than I could, even in my twenties when I was made high priestess. I don't know why your mother couldn't do it, sometimes it skips a generation, but my mother could do it, my grandmother as well, and even my great grandmother I vaguely remember, slowly doing the dance around the fire in her nineties."

Samantha rolled her eyes, thinking, "Here we go again," while grandma rued the skepticism on Sam's face.

"Look," grandma continued, "You may get stronger feelings of this sort as time goes on. You can tell me, it's fine. The others won't understand, they can't understand. You know the ritual is to protect the island and the earth from the void. What you saw yesterday evening, after the ritual, was the void fighting back."

Samantha let out a guffaw, incredulous.

Grandma continued undeterred. "I know it's hard to believe, but time will make you believe. I've been training you since you were a baby, and you're a natural. Just remember, if things get weird, return to the dance and the chant, preferably around a fire. The fire is the basis of your power, you can feed off it, harness it. Chant not the evocation, but the invocation next to a source of fire if you get scared. You remember the invocation?"

Samantha nodded. The invocation was beautiful. It was longer, like a story, melodic with slower dancing than the evocation. It was not done in front of large crowds, it was usually done in private, and she'd loved practicing it since she could walk. She remembered grandma doing it with her whenever she was sick, and she tended to do it out of habit when she was really worried, stressed out, or had cramps.

"You sure you remember?" grandma persisted.

"Yesss, of course," Sam said with a grimace, murmuring some lines as proof:

"Under the Earth, hot as Hades
My blood the magma boils
A vessel to hold my heat
Another mountain but oh so small
From within to without to within
My blood the magma boils
Not heat will burn
No fire will char
No lava will desecrate
Only will it consecrate
Burning away the useless
Clearing away the evil."

"That's right," grandma was pleased, "You'll do fine."

"Grandma, it's just song!" Samantha protested.

"No," grandma said, surprised the child couldn't feel it strongly enough yet. It had been ages since she'd first felt the awakening, the realization that she was connected to something more, in a way those around her were not. When had it been? Not til she was in her twenties. There were other priestesses, then, could that have delayed it? Here Samantha was barely a teenager, maybe she was too young. A similar storm had come when she was consecrated as high priestess. She must've already been 25, she was already married, could little Samantha already be drawing such power? She looked up the slope at the volcano, wondering, questioning, but the volcano was silent. She felt old, looking up, not up to her old duties, while the youthful cherub by her side was more than willing and able, doubting Thomas though she might be.

"No!" she replied again, more forcefully. "It's not just a song, and they aren't just words. It used to be sung in other dialects. If we go to Tahiti and elsewhere, you'd find it sung in different dialects. And you will see you have long-lost sisters, who perform the same dance, who sing the same chant, and thereby protect their people. You have to protect the island. You have to have daughters, and train them. It kills me that your mother didn't have any other girls."

She paused, realizing she was getting worked up and that this wouldn't help convince the child of the changes which were afoot. Calypso and Miranda were approaching with the clanging sound of a wheelbarrow full of tools.

"Look, let me tell you a quick story, and then we'll dig up some rocks and have guava smoothies with the others. The freak storm occurs every time a new high priestess is consecrated. Nobody was there to consecrate you, so it shouldn't have happened. The issue is that our power is weakest when we consecrate a new vessel, a new high priestess for Pele. The void seeks to destroy the island at these times."

"More stories of legend?" Calypso good-naturedly butted in.

"That's right, child, here can you help dump some of the rocks into the wheelbarrow? Too bad you don't have Kyle with you, he's got a good strong back that one," grandma added.

Then she continued, ignoring Miranda's rolling of eyes at the kids, Miranda having resolved long ago she couldn't get her mother to stop telling tales, finding it easier to humor her eccentricities.

"There are times when our defenses are lower, when the void can encroach. When my great grandma passed in November 1874, a huge storm came in. I was anointed High Priestess in August of

1950, and Hurricane Hiki slammed us. When the last other priestess died in September 1992 Hurricane Iniki blasted us, wiping out houses and more. Our defenses are low, and trouble could be in the works. Remember the chants, remember the dance, don't neglect to practice in the coming days, the void can sense you are new."

The wheelbarrow was almost full. Miranda was grimacing, and not from the lifting of rocks.

Calypso laughed and commented, "Just don't dance on the beach and calm the ocean too much, or Kyle won't catch any killer rides!"

"Indeed," said grandma seriously, "it is strange a child of the magma is so sympatico with one named after the sea."

They laughed and left the garden to have some smoothies and a couple musubi, Spam-topped sushi wrapped in a belt of seaweed, under the shade of a banyan tree on the other side of the house.

6 SICK AGAIN

They were down at the surf when the call came in. Samantha hadn't caught any decent rides in weeks, the waves kept petering out under her, like they do over uneven sand when there's a deep spot, they just lose steam. Other times, they'd just form and break too soon, almost like they were being blown out by the wind. Meanwhile, Kyle was catching rides around her, off with a "Booya!" on another wave. It was beautiful out on the water with a view of the beach, framed from behind with lush vegetation, tall trees with thick vines bearing leaves so large they looked like they were from a lotus field. Behind the forest, the low slopes of the hills gradually rose up to the looming ridges of the volcano in the background.

Volcano Priestess

Finally a big wave came in, and Samantha was in the right spot, early, before it got too tall so she could ride it on her hybrid 7' board. She started padding hard well before it reached her, getting up speed to catch it, and she gave a few kicks as it touched her feet to boost speed. The bloody wave formed too soon like the others, though, lifting her way up when she should've been shooting down the face at an angle like Kyle, or better yet shooting down, turning, and then jumping back over the top of the wave like a hot-shot shortboarder. Instead, she was on the top front edge. A little earlier, and she could've gotten a drop down onto the face, but maybe she hadn't paddled hard enough or her position was wrong, without her weight far forward enough on the board to go faster than the wave and get down on the face, instead she was in the unenviable position of gazing down about ten feet or so, mind you it looked like thirty feet, to the base of the wave, so clear you could see the coral reef under it, and as the wave broke she was thrown, not well-balanced on the board, down toward the base of the wave over the reef. She gasped as she fell, unsure how much water was over the reef.

Normally it was deep enough here, but the bigger waves pulled up a bunch of water in front. Samantha plunged down through the water over the reef, feeling thankful as she slowed some, but still she hit the reef with her hand, feeling it getting gouged as the water piled upon her, the pressure tumbling her, out of control. She was thankful it was her hand and not her head that hit the reef, yet unsure of where the surface was for a couple long seconds before she could make it

47

up, gasping for air. She looked at her hand; she'd lost a divot of flesh from one finger, no big deal, but it was going to hurt for a few days.

She was facing the shore, and could her the breaking water of the next roller coming in behind her. She barely had time to get another lung full of air before the wave hit and she went through the tumbler again, like she was in a washing machine with no air. As soon as the spinning was over, she figured out which way was up, and made it to the surface, she yanked on the surfboard leash connected to her ankle to pull the board to her. She could already hear the next big one coming in. She pulled herself onto the board and started paddling hard. She didn't want to get run through the washing machine again, it was nice being up top and able to breathe. All she had to do was get out in front far enough so the wave didn't crash down upon her, pushing her under with its weight back onto the reef.

In the back of her mind, she heard the lines, clear as she sang them around the fire, clear as grandma when she was a baby:

"Under the Earth, hot as Hades
My blood the magma boils…."

She could hear the water roaring behind her again, and she grunted as she paddled with both shoulders. Often beginning surfers thought they had to stick their hands down deep when paddling, but that was a waste of energy, fast and shallow, short sweeps of the arms was the way. The thundering crash behind her let her know she'd cleared the wave. She stopped paddling and held fast to the board, waiting for the broken wave's whitewash to carry her forward. It washed over her, lifting her up and blinding her in salty foam, catapulting her forward, while she leaned left and then right so she wouldn't flip over.

Coming up top she paddled a couple times to get further in front of the whitewash, and over its front edge she went, hopping up on the board in a fluid motion as she took off in front of the speeding foamy water. Stable on the board now, with a lot of water on the back, she was able to take a half step forward and turn the board some, so she arced left over the water toward her stuff on the beach. A feeling of elation filled her, jetting over the water almost like a bird taking flight. The wave covered a good hundred yards before petering out. It hadn't taken her all the way to shore, the break was too far out for that, but she made it a good distance and then, thinking she should tend her finger rather than roll the dice on catching more waves, she paddled into shore.

Back on the beach, she found the divot ripped from her finger was longer and deeper than she'd thought. Her finger was still numb, and it hadn't started bleeding yet, but she was sure it would. She grabbed a water bottle and dribbled fresh water on the wound to rinse it, and then stuck a napkin on it as a bandage, watching as Calypso shot down the face of a monster wave, disappearing temporarily into it as it started breaking over her shoulders, before shooting out the right side, up and over the back of the side of the wave.

"Go Calypso!" she thought as her friend paddled out to catch another. There was no point in yelling encouragement from the beach, it was just too loud out there in the surf. Moments later she saw Kyle catch the next wave, while close to shore, a few coconuts were pushed up out of the water onto the beach by a wave, only to languidly roll back into the water to ride again.

She debated going back in, but her shoulders were somewhat worn out, and it was harder to get up to speed and catch the waves when tired, so she blew it off. Instead, she donned some shades and leaned back to catch some rays. It was quite warm, and as she relaxed more, her finger didn't hurt any more, and she began wondering if a nap was in order, dropping off into a snooze.

In her dream it seemed she'd suddenly appeared at home, where the phone was ringing, and her mother was imploring her from the other room to get it, saying she was too busy with an amortization calculation. She awoke with a start. Of course she wasn't at home, she was napping on the beach. Calypso's phone had been ringing in the bag next to her.

She rolled over onto her side, digging it out of the bag to answer.

It was Calypso's mom.

"Esmeralda's sick, she's come down with something, can you guys come back and watch her? I need to go into work this afternoon, we have a regional meeting tonight," she told Samantha.

"Uh-huh, it'll take me a few minutes to get them out of the water, but we'll be back within an hour," Sam answered.

"Mahalo, that'll do, look forward to seeing you guys back here, gotta take care of the keiki."

Samantha really wasn't sure how to get them out of the water in short order; Kyle could surf for hours. Her name notwithstanding, Calypso wouldn't stay out that long. Like Samantha, her arms would tire, and she'd come in after an hour or two. She could try waving at them from the beach, but the break was out too far, they might not see and come in. So, she grabbed her board and paddled back out. Some of these reef breaks were way off shore, but this one was only about a quarter mile or so. Her finger stung in the salt water, but it wasn't like racing to catch a wave, she paddled out at an easy pace, using different muscles to mitigate the strain on her shoulders, by alternating between breast stroke and the more normal overhand paddling used for sprinting to catch waves. She stayed to the side where the waves weren't breaking, called the outside, and soon got their attention so they caught their last rides in.

Back at the house, Esmeralda was sicker than her mother had indicated. She was hacking up some serious phlegm, and running a temperature to boot.

"Calypso," she whined miserably, "I feel worse. It's like there's jellyfish in my lungs."

They checked the chunks of phlegm, they looked yellow. Usually the doctors prescribe antibiotics if you cough up colorful chunks, so they'd need their mother to take her into urgent care to get antibiotics prescribed later. Taking Esmeralda's temperature, Kyle found she was at 101.5°.

"Yup, she needs a doc," he commented, "Sorry Esmeralda, but you'll probably need two days for the meds to kick in, then you should be better. Dad's out of cell phone range, but we'll have mom take you as soon as she's back from her meeting tonight."

In the meantime, Calypso set up a humidifier in Esmeralda's room. Kyle's dad was gone, so there was nothing they could do but wait it out. Oddly, the wind was picking up, another freak squall, with gusts buffeting the house. You could hear the rain splash against the door and windows with the gusts. Also, the temperature was dropping. It was actually.....cold....like on the mainland, and as the rain poured harder the stream in the yard once again began to overflow.

They were watching TV and checking on the patient from time to time, when Kyle brought up the idea of BBQing some fish or chicken, or just nuking up some roasted pork leftovers and making rice. He wasn't afraid to get busy in the kitchen to feed the crowd. Samantha pointed out they should probably have something appropriate for the sick kid, though, like soup, maybe something fiery to help clear up the sinuses like dandan noodle soup. The others agreed, especially Calypso who loves Sam's quick dandan, a hybrid of dandan and gado-gado.

Samantha had Kyle boil up the noodles while she mixed cayenne, garlic, and fish sauce into a half cup of peanut butter, adding a spot of rice vinegar, water, and ginger at the end before nuking it to the point of boiling. While it was in the nuker she chopped some cabbage and green onions, rinsed some bean sprouts, and then threw the veggies in to nuke separately from the sauce. Similarly she nuked the roast pork leftovers separately, and then threw the soup together Asian-style, noodles first, then a light chicken and fish broth, then the cooked veggies and the pork, finally pouring a half cup of the thick red-tinted peanut sauce into the center of each bowl and topping them with green onions. Esmeralda loved her dandan, and sick though she was, she was happy to burn her throat clean with the spicy broth; she emerged from her room to eat soup on the couch as soon as she smelled the fumes wafting down the hall from the kitchen.

Kyle ate it the opposite way, not wanting to dilute the spicy goodness of the peanut sauce so he'd scoop it up thick with a giant Asian soup spoon out of the center of the bowl, whereas Esmeralda mixed the peanut sauce into the broth, fully diluting it so the whole thing was spicy instead of flaming hot in the center, mild broth on the outside ala Kyle.

Esmeralda was still coughing a lot, and sweating from the heat of the soup which made her nose run even more. The teens hoped she was OK, that it was helping to flush out the germs, as the theory goes. Esmeralda did sound better afterwards, with her sinuses flushed out, but she went back to bed for a nap even though it was only 7.

After a while, they checked her temp again, but now she was up to 103°, way too hot. Calypso was beginning to get worried now. This was too hot. She decided to call mom, but she wasn't answering, probably in the meeting, so Calypso texted her to come home now. The wind was getting worse, though, and when they looked out the stream had overflown the banks. In fact, the stream was now flowing on both sides of the house.

"There isn't even enough rain to make this happen," Calypso pointed out, incredulous. The islands are not known for dramatic weather; that's why it's called the Pacific Ocean. The nasty weather tends to get generated in the middle of the ocean and pack its punch not in the middle, but over in East Asia in the form of late summer and early fall typhoons, kind of like how the big hurricanes of the Atlantic form in the center, slam into the American east coast and the isles of the Caribbean, and leave Africa alone.

Samantha went in to check on Esmeralda, and found she was burning up. She took her temperature again and found she was up to 103.5°. This wasn't right. The rain wasn't right. The wind wasn't right. She walked out onto the porch. There was a river flowing around the house and down the street. Calypso's mom would never be able to drive up that in the car. There was so much water, bushes were leaning with the current, and a paint bucket floated by. The sight of the water made her sick to her stomach. She looked up at the sky, it was grey but the sky is grey a lot, and there was no way they should be able to get this much rain, not this fast, not even on Mount Waialeale on Kauai, which gets more rain than anywhere in the world.

She looked out over the ocean, and the ocean was dark. It was dark and unfriendly looking, and she could feel it mocking her. She could feel the mockery in the water all around her.

"No way..." she murmured to herself. She looked up at the volcano. "I don't believe in this," she said to the volcano. "I don't believe in this, and I don't believe in you!"

Calypso came out.

"What are we going to do? This is crazy. She's sick, and the road has turned into a river. We can't keep her here, if she gets any worse we'll have to throw her in the outrigger and try paddling her down the stream to a doctor."

Yes, Calypso was right, something needed to be done. Samantha felt herself grimacing, she couldn't believe this was actually happening.

"Put some ice in a towel and put it on her head," Samantha told Calypso. "You have to try to bring the fever down. Maybe the soup heated her up too much."

Calypso nodded.

"And have Kyle build a fire. A big fire, not a small one." Samantha added.

Calypso stopped and gave her a quizzical look. "A fire? But we need to cool her down, not heat her up."

Samantha felt better thinking about the flames. Yes, that was what they needed. They needed to fight all this water, all this unnatural water. There was no way this could be happening, and so there was only one way to fight it. With fire. She looked up at the volcano. She could see a dim red glow from the caldera, from the crater in the top. Was it really glowing? It was supposed to be covered in snow, still, with the pretty little lake. There were only spots of lava near the lake, the glow shouldn't be visible. But she didn't want snow and she sure didn't want water.

"The fire will warm her when the fever breaks and she gets the chills," she lied to Calypso, who looked unconvinced. The idea in of the fire burned within her. The water was still rising, there was nothing else they could do. Going in an outrigger was madness, the road was too steep, and outriggers aren't made for rapids, they aren't whitewater kayaks.

Sam strode into the house.

"Kyle, build me a fire to warm this pace up! It's too cold, we need to warm it up for Esmeralda, please do it now, and make it big."

She could feel the cold radiating from the walls, and she lit a candle just to fight the cold darkness. Calypso passed by with a towel and ice, heading into Esmerelda's room, while Kyle got a fire going in the living room.

The cheery flames filled the room with dim flickering orange light, casting shadows off the furniture near the fire.

The flames gave Samantha untold solace.

She started yanking one chair away from the fireplace.

"Kyle, help me move these out of the way, will you?"

It was his turn, now, to give Samantha a quizzical look.

"Umm, OK, I guess, but….why?" he asked tentatively, obviously thinking Samantha was going somewhat cuckoo.

"Um," she stammered, "It'll, um, help the air circulate so the house warms up more. You know how old fireplaces just don't work as well as wood stoves that get better air circulation around them, it's the same idea."

He looked skeptical, but helped drag the big heavy couch away from the fire.

She moved closer, seeing the kindling was spent and the middle-sized pieces of wood were really lighting up, such that the two big chucks of hardwood on top were starting to light.

The windows rattled with a gust, rain splashing across the pane.

That's enough out of you, Samantha thought. You'll get yours soon enough, blasted rain!

She threw open the chain mesh over the fireplace, and threw as much wood on the fire as would fit, kindling and mid-sized pieces and big pieces, she didn't structure it like she should, it was already burning and she just piles it on top, feeling the rising flames bolster her spirit.

She heard Calypso's footsteps behind her.

"What are you doing?" Calypso asked.

"I don't know…I mean, I do know, but it doesn't make sense," Samantha sputtered desperately.

"We're going to need to go soon," Calypso said. "Mom called and the road is flooded, she can't get back."

"Wait, give me a few minutes," said Samantha, standing tall in front of the fire, casting off her sweatshirt, and raising her hands over her head, fingers drooping down.

"What the…" said Calypso.

"I know, I know, it doesn't make sense, just let me try it, what's the harm?" Samantha said.

She began moving her hands high, careful to control the gestures of her fingers, she couldn't just wave them around, they had to turn and twist in the prescribed rhythm. She spun once and the words came without volition, without even trying to remember them, the prayer so ingrained, they sprang from her lips as though the words were not her own:

"Under the Earth, hot as Hades
My blood the magma boils
A vessel to hold my heat
Another mountain but oh so small
From within to without to within
My blood the magma boils
Not heat will burn
No fire will char
No lava will desecrate
Only will it consecrate
Burning away the useless
Clearing away the evil."

She moved with the dance, she could feel the fire within her, feel the rain draw back in fear. The volcano was with her and she would not be cold. Pele was with her and the rain would subside. The magma flowed within her veins and she would not be subsumed within the ocean or this river.

She continued the dance, and as she spun around, she could see the weather outside the window was already clearing. She caught her breath, shocked, elated, it was actually working. The dumb song, the dumb magic, it was somehow real and it was working. Her eyes were burning, maybe from the smoke, maybe from the realization, and she felt tears flowing down her cheeks as she continued into the evocation, feeling ever lighter on her feet as she chanted:

"Whatfore you were, whatfore thou shalt be
Heretofore I enforce thee
Heretofore I breathe into thee
The old falls away, burnt and expired,
Upon it we tread and grow
Na from Oha
Poi and ginseng
For all we provide
For all will fall burnt and expired
That we begin the circle anew."

There was a thunder clap overhead when she said the last word, "anew," and the whole house shook. She stopped and looked at the fire, burning brightly. Without the screen, embers had popped out onto the bricks, and she'd tracked soot all over in a circle, dancing in front of the fire. Her hands felt hot, it looked like there was steam coming off them.

The clouds had broken outside, the pink of sunset was reflected on their edges.

Kyle and Calypso were standing in the entrance to the room, mouths agape, looking at her.

"Wha----well, you know how fast our weather changes," Samantha blurted, "I'm sure it's a coincidence."

Kyle blinked dully at her. "I'll…. I'll go check on Esmeralda," he stuttered.

Calypso was crying. "This isn't right. That wasn't a coincidence. I can't believe this is happening. Let's go see Es," she added, and they dashed after Kyle.

Esmeralda was sitting up in bed drinking a Coke, Kyle grinning next to her.

"Feel her forehead you guys," he said to the girls, "her fever has broken."

Sure enough, they felt her forehead and the fever was gone. Calypso gave Sam a very grave, concerned look.

"I guess," Calypso said, looking into Sam's eyes, "I guess the ice on the head and the fire did work, after all," she said softly.

"I feel fine now, let's play death match challenge on the TV," quipped Esmeralda with a stuffy nose, and they all laughed.

Later that evening, when the flooding had subsided and Esmeralda's mom returned home to pronounced Esmeralda in fine health, Calypso again expressed her concerns to Sam.

"What's this all mean? Why did all that happen? What will happen next?" Calypso asked Sam when nobody else was around. Kyle laughed off the possibility that this was more than coincidence, saying weather on the ocean always changes fast, but Calypso knew what had transpired. She thought Kyle was in denial about the whole thing, but then she was more comfortable with ambiguity than he.

"I don't know, really," Sam answered weakly.

"C'mon, Sam, you know the legends. I didn't grow up with my grandma whispering those old tales in my ear, I don't really know what this means. I mean, I know it means you are some sort of sorcerer or something like that, but that's all I know. What's this mean? Is this the end, is something else going to happen?"

Samantha gazed through a window up at the mountain, up at the volcano, silent. What could it mean? She tried to remember the stories. There were so many, and they all seemed like things grandma just made up as she went, meaningless bedtime stories and rhymes. Except some of the rhymes had just changed the weather and healed a sick child like flicking a switch.

"What's it mean!?!" Calypso repeated desperately.

"I don't know, Cal, I don't know. I got to ask grandma. Will you come with me to see her after school tomorrow?"

"Sure thing, you bet, sister!" Calypso answered, and Samantha felt a little better, if still shell-shocked.

7 INVOCATION

"The only thing we have to fear is fear itself"
Franklin Delano Roosevelt, during first inauguration speech as US
President, Saturday, March 4, 1933

In the morning, Esmeralda was fine, and insisted on going to
school to tell her friends about the weird storm and her sudden
recovery, over her mother's protestations. Samantha still felt her
fingers tingle, and wondered if the fire had burned her. Once as a
girl her hands and legs had blistered after dancing too long with
grandma around a very large bright fire during a late night luau party.
It had happened again from doing the same kind of dances at a fiesta
party some neighbors from Mexico threw one time, complete with a

piñata for the kids. Samantha remembered being disappointed she couldn't even hit the piñata, being sullen as she returned to dance with grandma around the fire, away from the other kids, while later being appreciative since so many of the ladies complimented her on her dancing. Oddly, one of them called it "folk dancing."

Only now did she know that to them, it was folk dancing, and while she didn't like the term at the time, that's all it was to her as well. But now she knew it most certainly was not a quaint meaningless folk dance, whatever it may appear to be. Only now did she understand that the way she held her hands, the accuracy of her chant, all this made it so much more. She felt her hands tingle again as she thought about it. Weird.

After school they took the bus home up the mountain, grabbed their bikes and some bottles of water, and started the long route to grandma's house. It was late afternoon by the time they made it there.

Grandma was tottering about in the garden as usual. They could hear her calling as they approached, as though she knew they were on their way. Maybe Miranda had tipped her off they'd be coming.

Grandma had a fistful of flowers in one hand, exclaiming, "You did it! You did it!"

"Did what?" Calypso responded with a grin, somewhat bewildered.

"Well, the evocation, of course, her first successful complete evocation!"

Samantha nodded, grimly, not thinking this was such a good occasion after all. It was nice when this was a fun family tradition. It was not so nice when it turned the weather against her and almost killed her best friend's little sister, someone she'd known since a baby, practically a keiki of her own ohana.

Now that she was here, she wasn't sure what to say. Grandma looked at her, and she looked at grandma. The words, the tales, of all these last 13 years, they all made sense. What was there, really, to ask? She'd been given the answers already. She knew the answers. The problem was believing it all. Had she gone crazy? Was this really real? She needed to hear it again. She needed to hear it direct from her grandmother.

"I never believed," she started out helplessly. "I don't understand."

"I know, sweetie, the first evocation is scary, the first time you feel the spirit."

"But I don't get it, how can this be real?"

Grandma just smiled. "It is as it has always been. I don't know when it started, I don't know how far this goes back, but it's always been in the family. I was shocked too, my first time, but of course I was used to hanging out with the priestesses, and there were a lot of us back then, it's not just our family you know, there are others, but some like your mother turned away from the path or were never suited for it."

Samantha was still dumbstruck, but Calypso still had her wits about her.

"So, what's this mean, is, like, you know, the rain or ocean trying to get her or something?"

"Come inside and I'll explain more," grandma said, and soon they were all having sodas around the kitchen table.

"It's not as though the weather is sentient and after you," grandma explained. "It's more that there is a void created by my retirement." She cleared her throat, seeing the girls just looked even more confused. "When you successfully performed your first evocation the other night, you sent me into retirement. I can still back you up, but you've started to become the high priestess. If it was earlier, if I was younger, I'd still retain my power longer, but at my age I just can't pull it all off. For you to fully succeed me as high priestess, you'll need to successfully perform the invocation, actually making Pele come forth."

"Come forth?!?!" Samantha repeated. "Grandma what the heck does that mean? I don't want the rain and floods to kill anyone, and I sure don't want Pele appearing, whatever that means."

Grandma laughed. "You already made Pele's spirit manifest itself, your first big step in protecting the island from the water and the sea. They'll wear the island away to nothing without us, you know. As the evocation summons the spirit of Pele outside of you, the invocation brings Pele within your body. It's not like you summon some flaming fire goddess who runs around burning everything down or anything like that, don't worry, when I first did the invocation, I just held hands with some other priestesses and walked across a bed of charcoal. With the fire within me, I could no longer be harmed by the heat."

"What's that, she'll be, like, immune to fire?" Calypso squealed, incredulous.

"Um," said grandma, "I guess so, kind of, while doing the invocation anyway, I mean I'm not sure it's so simple, you kind of have to feel your way through what you can do and can't do."

"Immune to fire?" Samantha murmured after them. Could it be true? She remembered the ember on her foot from the night she ascended the slope to dance the dawn. She'd assumed it was an anomaly that it didn't burn her, but she knew now what grandma was getting at.

"Here, let's light a candle," grandma said, glancing through the window up at the volcano.

"But why would this threaten my sister?" Calypso explained. "She doesn't have anything to do with this."

Grandma didn't respond at first, pondering the matter as she lit the candle.

Samantha's eyes grew wide. Fire didn't look the same as it used to. It wasn't just there, she felt connected to it somehow, as though its warmth flowed from her.

"It's not after your sister," grandma explained. "The weather is reacting to the emptiness on the island, the void of volcano power, it's trying to take the island back, to sink it under the ocean. Samantha is the only one who can protect the island now."

Grandma held her hand over the fire for ten long seconds. The smoke came out from either side of her palm.

"Take your hand back," exclaimed Calypso, "You'll get burnt."

Finally she grimaced and pulled her hand back, soot all over her palm. She rubbed off the soot and there was only a small red spot.

"My connection grows weak," grandma commented, as Calypso tried it.

After about a second Calypso started growling in pain, and then after another second she yanked her hand back, clearly burnt much worse than grandma who'd held her hand over the flame for some five times more.

"Boy that hurts!" exclaimed Calypso, "OK, high priestess," she said with a giggle and a raised eyebrow, "let's see you do it better than grandma!"

Samantha didn't find it amusing. This was messed up. Even if she could withstand an ember, or a candle, that didn't mean she could turn the weather or protect the islands. She was 13, she was barely in a position to get a B on the math quiz at the end of the week. She was in no position to protect the islands from anything.

She looked at the flame, thinking about its warmth. She could sense it, from across the table. It wasn't a bonfire, yet she could feel the warm on her face. She held out her hands toward the flame, not getting too near it, and she could feel the warmth. In the back of her mind, she could hear the chant. She stood up, holding her hands over her head, and she could feel the warmth inside her chest. Yes, this was feeling the flame, it was not really about physically touching it.

She started moving around the table, making the hand signs of the dance over her head as she moved, beginning the invocation:

"Under the Earth, hot as Hades
My blood the magma boils
A vessel to hold my heat
Another mountain but oh so small
From within to without to within
My blood the magma boils
Not heat will burn
No fire will char
No lava will desecrate
Only will it consecrate
Burning away the useless
Clearing away the evil."

The candle was burning more brightly now, brighter than she'd ever seen a candle burn, the fire several inches high, the wax running down over the candlestick all over the table, and Samantha stuck her hand right in it. She held it there, repeating the invocation, more slowly, easing down into her chair.

Her hand felt hot, that was certain, but then so did her other hand, so did her face, she could feel the flame within her, and it felt hotter than the candle. It was almost as if the candle was cooler, was even cooling her hand off. She held up her other hand, which felt hotter than the one in the flame, she held it in front of her face and wiggled the fingers, which felt stiff. Her hand seemed to be glowing, almost, or maybe it was a reflection in the room.

"It doesn't hurt?" Calypso asked.

"No…it almost feels good somehow, like it's one of those fake flame lamps with flames made of paper moved by a fan," Samantha said slowly.

"OK, well, maybe it's OK for me, too!" Calypso added, stretching her hand out toward the abnormally large candle flame.

Grandma opened her mouth to protest, but Calypso snatched her hand back right quick.

"Shoot, it's way hotter than it was before," Calypso exclaimed. "What about your hand, is it, like, cool or is it the same temperature as the flame?"

"You shouldn't touch my hand," Samantha answered automatically. Somehow she felt instinctively, her hand would be too hot. The longer she touched the fire, the more she felt one with it, and different from Calypso.

Samantha still had one hand in the fire, while she reached with the other hand toward Calypso's hand. The air was cool around Calypso's hand, too cool, like a cold breeze was coming off Calypso's fingers.

"No way!" Calypso exclaimed, "Your hand is like an oven, I can feel the heat coming off it!" She turned to grandma. "Doesn't this mean that she's successfully performed the invocation, that we're now safe?"

Grandma smiled weakly, while the girls looked at her expectantly. "Well, this is certainly a promising start. I wouldn't say Samantha's reached the apex of her powers as a high priestess, though, we have to give her time to get better at this, to get stronger."

Samantha started to speak but Calypso burst in. "How? When? Esmeralda got really sick the other day, and we have to prevent that from happening again! How do we know when it will be safe?"

Samantha looked doubtfully at her grandma, who returned her

look with a reassuring expression.

"Mastery comes through practice, dears. She needs to do the dance. With the lack of other high priestesses, it's probable her power will again be challenged. For the safety of the rest of the family, you should probably move in with me for a few days, or into your aunt's house."

Samantha gasped. Miranda wouldn't even let her visit her aunt's former abode. In fact, she thought it was burned to the ground, subsumed in lava and ash.

"I thought it was too dangerous up there," she replied.

"It is, for keiki. It is, for Calypso and Kyle. It is, for your mother. But it is not, not for you and not for me. Wait a day or two, practice the dance, and then you and I will go there together. I'll call your mother, and tell her I'm sick and need you to watch over me for a couple days."

"She'll be suspicious."

"Yes, of course, she'll be suspicious, but she'll relent. Don't worry, I'm her mother, I'll convince her." She smiled kindly. Miranda was a good kid. She just didn't have the aptitude to defend the island, but she was a good kid. Soon, she'd recognize her progeny was strong with the family traditions, and she'd come to respect both her mother, and her daughter more. Less accounting, more magic.

8 POSSESSION

The girls took off around 7PM or so. Samantha felt like the caldera was watching her, not like a teacher or someone evaluating her actions, more like a protective parent, standing in the background, waiting in case intervention was necessary. It was weird, the whole thing was weird, really too weird to believe.

Most of the way back was downhill on dirt roads. They went fast, periodically skidding on the gravel in the curves, or catching some air off small bumps. Once they got back on the paved roads, they rode so fast their bikes vibrated with the speed, tires wobbling under them like they had turned to jelly. Were they going all the way into town, they'd have had to slow down for the speed trap where the highway patrolman sometimes camped out with a radar gun, since they were assuredly going over the 25 MPH speed limit that applied to all the back roads.

They were back by around 8. Miranda had promised to bring some kalua pork back from town for dinner, an occasion for which Kyle showed up, happy to work a "second dinner" into his busy schedule of surfing and homework. They had big piles of rice with the kalua pork, which actually has no coffee-flavored Kahlua in it, the cooked cabbage it always comes with, and some salad topped with a bit of shrimp and sliced mango. Good mango is creamy, if not quite as much as avocado, but with a touch of citrusy aftertaste.

They briefed Kyle on meeting grandma while Miranda was out of the room. Needless to say Kyle was more than a tad skeptical that his childhood friend was a divine agent, purportedly immune to fire. He'd always known Samantha was special and liked her more than any other girl, but that she was imbued with magic was harder to swallow than a conch shell.

Miranda came in the room with a cell phone in her hand.

"Why didn't you tell me your grandmother was ill?!?!" she demanded.

"Sorry, Mom, I figured she should ask you," Samantha replied, as

Kyle lit a candle in the middle of the table.

"What's that for?" Miranda asked, for some reason looking annoyed by the presence of the candle.

"Oh, uh, just atmosphere, I guess. Grandma always likes candles, I thought?" Kyle replied disingenuously. Calypso, her back to Miranda, was smirking. Kyle was looking for a demonstration.

"Yeah, OK, well fine, go there after school tomorrow, and keep us appraised. I mean, I don't see why she won't just go see a doctor if she thinks she's so sick she needs you there as her caretaker."

"I know, Mom, it seems weird, but on the other hand it just seems like she's under the weather. You know how damp it's been recently, she says it makes her joints hurt and stuff like that. I guess it's just part of growing old, hopefully they'll have a cure for that by the time I'm that old."

"If you ask me," Miranda quipped, "it's all that bloody dancing she does. Sure, she's fit for her age, but no wonder she has joint problems. When I was a kid it was constant, her and all her friends dancing and chanting all the time, and they always seemed to have candles like that one around," she added suspiciously.

"Anyway," Miranda continued, "I suppose it's fine, just ring us up and let us know how things are going a couple times this weekend, OK? I hate that she won't get a cell phone given how often her land line seems to be out of service. I mean, what a Luddite."

"Yeah, OK," Samantha replied, not knowing a Luddite was someone who opposes technical progress, "Thanks Mom, I'll call you on Saturday and update you."

Miranda left the room to watch TV with Samantha's dad, and Kyle didn't have any trouble convincing Samantha to repeat her performance of earlier in the afternoon.

"I'm supposed to practice a lot anyway, but just don't tell anybody, OK, they'll think I'm some sort of crazy freak," Sam said to Kyle.

Once again she did a chant, not real loud lest her parents hear, and held her hand in the flame til her shoulder got tired from leaving it there. It almost seemed like it felt better and better, the longer she held it in the flame, with the chant running through her head even though she didn't bother to actually speak the words after the first couple times saying it aloud.

Kyle's eyes had grown wide when she stuck her hand in the flame. As with Calypso, he also touched the flame briefly in disbelief, and inspected her hand for damage afterwards, once it had cooled down since it glowed for a while after she removed it from the flame.

"My friend the fire witch," he joked. "Can you summon fire or fire elementals or anything like that?" he asked.

"Of course not, silly, I have no idea how I'm supposed to do anything, just because my hand doesn't burn isn't going to do anything to save the island, I really don't get it….."

She was quiet for a moment. "What if my grandma is just crazy?" she finally said.

Calypso looked shocked. "She's not crazy. Look at what you just did! Isn't that proof enough?"

"What if I'm crazy, what if this is all a dream? I mean, wouldn't that make more sense? People just aren't immune to fire, we all know that, we're mostly made of water."

Kyle nodded. "Yeah, it doesn't seem to make sense. Bu like Cal says, the proof's right here. You guys aren't nuts. Maybe your bodies have special sweat glands that allow you to withstand the heat. You know water is supposed to boil off your skin before the skin gets burned, something like that, or like how people walk across beds of coals."

Samantha smiled. "I guess maybe there is a scientific basis for this. That would be comforting. Still, don't tell anybody, OK?"

"Sure, OK Samantha," they agreed, and Kyle went for seconds on the pork and rice, adding some yellow takuan pickle slices on top of the rice since they were out of kimchee.

After school the next day, Samantha rode up to grandma's. She was happy to hang out with grandma, but she didn't feel comfortable at all about the prospect of going to auntie's house, or whatever ruins might be left there. It seemed creepy.

Grandma told her not to worry about all that for now, though. Someone had delivered a cord of wood, dumped out of a pickup in a big messy pile on the driveway. She and Samantha started porting it out into the field of volcanic rocks, a couple logs at a time, to a fire pit grandma used in the past for cooking large amounts of food for parties, back when the family lived with her. She didn't throw big parties anymore, but came down to Miranda's for them instead.

"Nobody else is around, so we're going to practice with real fire now," she said to Samantha, who didn't follow her meaning, but soon would. They got a small fire burning as the sun set, going over the horizon without much fanfare, hardly any clouds around to pick up the colors. Then they practiced the dances together, gradually building the fire larger. At one point they had a huge bed of coals.

"Go ahead and stick your hand in," grandma said.

"Is it safe?" Samantha asked, knowing what the answer was, and finding it out for herself by grabbing a small glowing ember. She giggled, while grandma gave her a bored look.

"Look, I know you're still getting warmed up, but try this," grandma said, sticking her hand right into the bed of coals, halfway up to her elbow. Samantha watched, expecting her to pull the hand back out, but she just let it sit there, for at least 20 seconds, before looking bored and pulling it out.

Samantha found she could copy her. It hurt at first, she thought, or perhaps she just thought it hurt since it should've hurt. They did the dance some more, repeating the evocation and then the invocation, and eventually danced barefoot on the bed of coals as the fire died down.

"You're a natural," grandma said, "most young priestesses take til their mid-twenties to reach your level of ability. I guess I did start training you earlier than normal, though. Tomorrow, we'll practice some more and then go to auntie's house."

The next morning, Samantha found grandma was already awake and in the garden when she awoke. She toasted a bagel with ham and cheese for Sam, and gave her a cup of jasmine tea.

"Let's go back to the fire pit," she told Samantha.

"But there's no wood left, we burned through it all," Samantha replied, hoping they wouldn't have to repeat the exercise of carrying another pile of wood into the field.

"Yes, well, let's see what we find," grandma said.

Walking across the field, it was obvious what they'd find; there was still a prodigiously healthy column of smoke rising from the coals. It wasn't surprising to Samantha, they'd burned though a huge amount of wood the night before, something like a half cord. Her arms were still tired from lugging it back and forth, while her fingertips felt dry and light, and the skin cracked and red, but her fingers felt full of energy, like they wanted to wiggle about, like they wanted to lead her in the dance. Her legs seemed to feel the same way, yearning for the dance, full of energy. Only the arms felt like the logs they carried, heavy and immutable.

When they reached the fire pit she didn't wait for grandma to say anything, her fingers seemed to lead the way. She started the graceful motions, gesturing with her forefingers toward her third eye before making a sweeping motion with her hands to clear the air before her, then prancing forward bending and extending her fingers with her hands held aloft, gradually forgetting the tired forearms and biceps as either breakfast or the dance made the energy flow.

She wondered why the pit was still so hot; it should have been dying out but it seemed to be gaining in intensity as she recited the evocation.

A light breeze flowed over the volcanic slope. Samantha gazed far away, over the fields, down the hills, over the forest out over the water, the cold deep water. We are not children of the water, she thought to herself. The water provides fish but cannot sustain us. She wanted to ask her grandma why that was, she wanted to ask her why the pit was still hot, but as she continued the dance she felt she need not ask grandma. The fire would provide the answer.

She could feel heat waves in the air around her making things blurry, like the waves of heat far off on a highway making a mirage appear. Her fingers were getting hotter and hotter as she proceeded with the invocation, drawing the spirit of the fire within her. Grandma was sitting on a rock on the side, happily chanting along with her, but not dancing. Samantha felt heat coming from her grandmother, as well as the fire pit, and she now felt somewhat possessed, not like there was a sentient demon spirit inside her or something creepy like that, but as though a foreign heat source was inside her. It was a pleasant feeling, like the warmth of drinking hot cocoa in the snow, spreading through one's innards and out to one's arms and legs.

The fire pit was hotter now, and she understood what was going on. She was summoning the magma from below. A normal bonfire would be petering out by now, but they had summoned magma. Growing up on a volcano, Samantha knew that meant a fissure had formed under them. She felt its power surging through her. She should have been fearing for her life, but instead she was filled with exuberant joy. She stopped skipping about the fire, spinning once as she came to a halt, splaying her fingers out in front of her over the fire. They were glowing, yellow orange heat coming from within. She laughed and gleefully grabbed a handful of coals from the edge and flung them up into the air, stepping briskly into the dull red fire, finding it felt like cool mud on her feet, grey ash over thick molten material. It was thick like clay mud, with granules she could feel like sand between her toes.

Kicking her foot up she splashed the molten rock out of the pit, thick chunks of lava sticking to the rocks they hit, and glowing for a moment as they cooled. It was exhilarating, like splashing in the surf, but this material was her friend, she felt she could control it. It wouldn't smoosh her into a coral reef. No shark or giant squid hid in its depths. It was clean, pure, and formed islands for the people. It made the fields which made the food. It captured the water for them to drink. There was no drinking the salt water. The caldera and volcano would catch the rainwater, would filter the water, would

Volcano Priestess

support the people. She gave a shriek of joy, feeling the truth wash over her, kicking more molten lava up out of the pit, laughing as it splashed on rocks and sizzled through the few tufts of grass it hit.

"Grandma, come in and play, it feels great," she said.

Grandma smiled benevolently, but shook her head no. Samantha rolled her hips back and forth, extending out her arms again, palms flat to the ground, raising and lowering her arms like they were wafting in the wind, feeling more and more heat coming from under her.

She clapped her hands, happy as a clam, and the earth shook violently under her, so she stumbled. The lava was bubbling now, the stench of sulfur smelling like the Fourth of July. The hotter the fire grew, the more it seemed to draw gusts of wind. The bubbling magma looked as friendly as chicken soup simmering on the stove, but the tremors under her gave her pause. Was she causing this, or was it a coincidence? She didn't want to make it erupt or anything, they were only a hundred feet or so off from grandma's house. Strange though it was that the lava wasn't burning her, she wasn't at all convinced the house would be immune.

She stopped cold.

"Grandma, is this what happened to auntie? Did she summon the lava? Why did it hurt her? Didn't she know the evocation? Didn't she chant the invocation?"

Grandma's eyes grew dark. She had never liked talking about this topic, but of course there was no getting out of it this time, this was a key part of Samantha's tutelage. She had to know the truth. Grandma had prepared for this for decades. She'd taken no chances with Samantha, teaching her the dances since she was two years old. All little Samantha knew was that bottles of milk and later candy went together with the dance. Grandma had tried every Pavlovian trick she could think of to keep the child motivated to do the gestures, to learn the words.

"I'll explain when we get there. Come out of the lava and have a seat, rest for a spell, let yourself cool down."

She could see some smoke coming off her fingers, and she sat down and tried to cool down, but the fire was within her and it didn't want to leave, it didn't want to cool down. It was sad to drive it away, to return to normal.

"Can't I just stay warm, I like it," Samantha said, not wanting to cool down.

"I can't take you to aunties like that, you'd burn right through the seat cushions in the jeep," grandma said, a smile playing about the corners of her lips.

Samantha sat for a while, walked around the field to kill time while cooling off further, and she felt the warmth subside slowly, her fingers ceasing to glow after a couple minutes, the hot feeling then leaving her extremities though her belly and chest still felt warm.

She was thirsty but grandma said she mustn't drink water for at least 20 minutes, explaining that she was too hot inside and it would bubble up in steam as frighteningly powerful burps, that could even be dangerous for her stomach if she was still flaming hot.

Finally they had miso soup with clams and rice on the side, and then went to auntie's house, reputedly destroyed in the lava flows. Grandma brought some camping gear, explaining that they'd spend the night there, and return on Sunday. Samantha put in a call to Miranda as they drove, telling her they were fine and that she'd call on Sunday.

The more she cooled down, the more tired she seemed to be.

"Wow," she said as they drove, "all that dancing really took it out of me."

"That's fine, sweetie, go ahead and take a nap, I'll wake you when we get there."

9 THE JOY OF LAHAR

They stopped near a big field of black hardened mud. Grandma explained that this was the remains of the lahar, a landslide of mud and volcanic debris. They scrambled over about a half mile of the stuff before reaching a trough that opened up, about 30 feet deep, extending down the hill in a narrow gully. The top of the trough held a burnt-out trailer home, charred plastic and rusted metal twisting upwards like it had been hit by Japanese bombs back during the war.

"That's it," grandma said flatly, a grim look on her face.

Miranda had told Samantha not to ask her grandmother about this event. Evidently grandma stopped speaking after her eldest was killed, only starting to speak again after a very distant cousin visited from Aogashima when her husband passed some three years later. Miranda had refused to send her to a hospital, though, and let the elders summon the lady from southern Japan to help, whose incessant chanting eventually appeared to wake grandma from her reverie, for her lips started mimicking those of the Japanese high priestess, quivering with the words at first, eventually forming them again until she was fully chanting, and actually speaking within a few days.

They scrambled down the steep gritty edge of the gully.

"Evangelique was a talented but spoiled child," grandma mused. "She moved up here to be closer to the volcano. She always wanted to summon the magma up, to send the lava flying. She wanted to grow the island, and kept working on her invocations. Miranda just couldn't do it, even though she tried harder than Evangelique."

Grandma paused, looking at the ground, idly making lines in the dust with the edge of her sandals.

"This spot has had fissures nearby, so the land was dirt cheap, and Evangelique figured it was the perfect place for summonings."

"So what happened?" Samantha asked after a long pause.

"Well," grandma continued with a sigh, "Your aunt was never a careful practitioner. She always was interested in how much lava she could summon, but she did it in an evocation style, trying to control it without welcoming it within her."

Grandma cast her a sharp glance.

"You can't control it that way. Just because you can make it appear doesn't mean you can control it."

Samantha was confused. She didn't feel like she could control it either.

"I made it appear, but it didn't hurt me. Isn't that the same?" Samantha asked, wondering if she needed to be worried. While she had the heat within her, she couldn't have conceived of it hurting her, but on the other hand, she had just made a pit full of lava, not a whole field.

"You're better at the invocation," grandma said, "and through no accident at all, you've been practicing for about 11 years."

She cleared her throat.

"I myself was probably guilty of hubris. I was so convinced of Evangelique's abilities that I didn't make her practice enough. She would practice a fair amount, sure, but her dancing was a little sloppy and all too often she had Motown music blasting in the background. It's no wonder she couldn't achieve mastery over the invocation."

"How do you know I'm any better?" Samantha exclaimed. "What if I trigger something like this lahar, just like auntie?"

"Auntie's fingers never glowed," grandma said with a gleam in her eye.

"Auntie never ran the mountain and danced the dawn," she said with a sad look, a couple tears coming first from her left eye and then also her right.

"I let her be borne into this life, but I didn't force the discipline upon her to control it correctly. I thought she had it all under control, and was making good progress, but look at this," she gesticulated at the walls of the gully around her.

"She summoned enough magma to create a small volcanic dome up on the slope, and the resulting melting of snow washed over this whole area." Grandma picked up a softball-sized rock, shaped like a giant almond with grooves running along its length.

"This is a lava bomb," grandma said, "from flying lava that cools in the air." She tossed it to Samantha.

"Wow, it's heavy."

"These are what destroyed the trailer," grandma said. "Evangelique could mostly protect herself, though nothing like you, but the trailer and your uncle are two different matters altogether. They were both destroyed by falling lava, while the poisonous gasses overwhelmed your aunt."

Grandma's frame shook with sobs as she recounted the end of the tale. "I was not afraid of the volcanic mudslide, the lahar. I of course was stronger back then, stronger than Evangelique, and I could feel the earthquakes down at my house, stuff was coming off the shelves and onto the floor everywhere."

She waved at Samantha to follow her, and walked over to the ruins of the trailer, tears running down her face.

"The lahar was still wet, of course, and though I tried to walk over it, it was too thin, like wading through rocky quicksand, but after a few hours your grandpa found the entrance to this gully way down below." She pointed to a burnt-out chair frame in the middle of the trailer, holding her hand up, trembling.

"She was in that chair when I found her, her head bent back in a strange way, rain falling all over as though the ocean was reclaiming her from us."

She dropped her hand and slumped down onto the ground, pulling her legs up under her. She pulled a juice packet out of her thigh pocket and tossed it to Samantha.

"Losing Evangelique destroyed me," she said. "I would still dance, but I couldn't chant, and I couldn't speak, not even to your grandpa. Evangelique was being counted upon to recruit a new generation of priestesses for the island."

She drank it, still thirsty from earlier, and then they practiced the evocation. Gathering some kindling, they made a small fire and practiced the invocation. It wasn't long before the ground was glowing red-hot again, and as Samantha once again was filled with joy, she began to wonder why auntie had resisted, why she hadn't taken the fire within her. She began to wonder if she needed any fire to summon the magma, to make it pour forth from the earth in streams of lava. Over the course of the day they made several small fires in different spots of the gully, performing the evocation and invocation each time, and Samantha felt herself getting stronger and stronger, finding the feeling of being possessed by the flame was stronger each time, and took less time and dancing to achieve.

The crescent moon was slowly moving across the sky as they continued practicing into the night, leaving hot glowing spots all around the gully. Finally they inflated some backpacking mattresses and went to sleep, and Samantha dreamed first she was a candle, later she was the sun, buried under the earth, trying to get out, to get free and express herself, yearning to burst forth from under the heavy layers of rock and water lying above.

10 TSUNAMI

When they awoke Sunday morn, the sky was dark with thick clouds. Clouds are attracted to the low pressure zones around tropical islands, but these weren't innocuous thin clouds. These were towering thunderheads.

Grandma looked warily at the sky. "When you are older, be sure to train more high priestesses, and then there won't be so much trouble during periods of transition like this. If Evangelique was alive, this wouldn't be so bad. Sure, there would be rain, but nothing dangerous, nothing this bad."

"How will I do that, grandma?"

"You'll eventually need to devise a plan for figuring out who has the talent, and recruit them. The Tahitian high priestess said she does it by masquerading as a luau dance teacher while recruiting fire-breathers who dance with the fire. She just tests if they seem to take to the dance readily, and if they do, she teaches them an initial chant while having them handle fire. She said you could tell in short order who has the knack for it and who doesn't, for example who passes the flaming torch right under their arm slowly without pain, to illustrate who's becoming immune to the fire."

"What, so I have to run a luau school for thousands of children just to find a couple priestesses?" Samantha retorted, not liking the idea at all. Working for a big hotel doing luau for loud tourists was her idea of a nightmare job. She'd rather work the front desk or clean toilets or work in accounting like her mother.

"I'm not saying you should do this," grandma chided her, "It was just her idea, what she was doing. Besides, she doesn't do the luaus, she just does training, while promoting traditional dance and culture. Sure, the hotels love it since they get better quality dancers, but the idea is to promote traditional culture and the traditional dance, rather than dance moves made up by somebody the hotel hires fresh out of New York or Los Angeles dance school."

Samantha thought about this for a minute. "That would be more like being one of those moms who runs swim lessons out of her backyard," Samantha mused. "I could post fliers up around school and give lessons, maybe Calypso would help and we could make some money for college." Samantha was always worried about tuition costs, no doubt since Miranda talked about college funds and paying off the mortgage so she could go on her dream vacation to Italy all the time.

"Part of the key," grandma added, "Is to go after a more traditional demographic. It's not that there's anything wrong with the haole kids, I'm no racist, but pure haoles never become priestesses, it's not in their blood. Even a millionth Polynesian will suffice; I hear in Tahiti there's even a platinum blonde high priestess. This lady is immune to fire like any other high priestess. Nonetheless, she still has to wear extra sunscreen all the time, immunity to fire is one thing, not being able to tan is another." They both laughed.

"Seriously, though, you need to continue training every night, even if you just dance around a candle in your room, until these clouds go away and things return to normal."

Samantha remembered Esmeralda getting sick, and wanted things to get back to normal as quickly as possible. Discussing the dance training plan later with Calypso, she was surprised Calypso was into it.

"This would be a perfect way for us to make money this summer!" Calypso vaunted, and before long they had a flier designed for "Calypso and Sam's Ocean Luau Classes, beginner and up. Fire-breathing training for qualified applicants only." Even Kyle got interested in the idea, thinking he could run classes in outrigger paddling and fishing for kids.

"This way, the parents can drop off both their boys and their girls," Kyle pointed out, "So you're likely to get more customers. You aren't really thinking you're going to get a bunch of boys in your luau classes, are you," he scoffed. "Anyway, if you do that's fine, but the burly ones can come get outrigger and fishing training with me. Dad will love this idea, all the stuff he's taught me, I can teach to others."

As it turned out, dad didn't love the idea, dad turned out to be more concerned about the insurance premiums to protect the family from any lawsuits launched by students' parents.

"Have to have liability insurance, indemnification," he quipped, "Otherwise you'll be in deep do-do if some kid twists her ankle and the parents sue. You may not see this in the village so much, but in Hilo or bigger cities, there are attorneys who specialize in this sort of thing."

Nevertheless, after school the next day he took them along on a shopping run up to Hilo, so they could post their fliers all the way up and down highway 137. He also bought a liability insurance policy at a discount online.

Back in the village that evening, they stopped for some teriyaki chicken rice bowls on the way home. It was raining heavily, and Samantha was feeling guilty she'd not done a dance since the AM. Each time she danced, the weather seemed to clear up.

She was slurping down a soda with a skewer of chicken and green onions in one hand when the tsunami warning sirens started going off. She felt her stomach cinch up with fear immediately. Here on the southeast side of the island, these sirens were deadly serious. She looked out to sea; fortunately it looked calm, so hopefully it wasn't the Hilina Slump. Right off the coast, the land dropped off steeply, for too steep and far too deep, formed by the volcano over the millennia. It wasn't formed of solid rock, though, and parts were bound to settle over time, in the form of underwater landslides. We're not talking about a small landslide of an area like a single yard around a single house, we're talking about a 5,000 cubic mile section, bigger than a city, plunging thousands of feet into the ocean. The geologists think it's happened before since the dinosaurs, and it's likely to happen again in the next 100,000 years, but whether it will be gradual in small chunks, or one giant event, they just don't know. If one giant event, the tsunami could be over a thousand feet high. Samantha and Calypso knew these facts well, living on one of the largest volcanos on the planet, next to one of the worst tsunami zones on the planet.

She still had the skewer in one hand as they jumped into the truck and Kyle's dad blasted uphill. He was normally a conservative guy, one who always took life jackets, obeyed the speed limit, and didn't cheat on his taxes.

"Cheating ruins the game," he said, like it was axiomatic to life.

But he didn't like the idea of losing his oldest two kids to a tsunami, not one bit, he couldn't do that to his wife. And he didn't want to leave the world quite yet, either. The truck groaned as he kept the pedal down, tires squealing around a leafy corner on the hill. There was a stop sign ahead, but he slammed his foot on the gas instead of the brake.

"Dad," Calypso implored, "Don't kill us to save us!"

"I ain't messing around!" he retorted. "I'll cry about the speeding ticket I get if I get one, but better crying about a speeding ticket than being sucked out to sea and killed," he said. They all knew they lived in the world's worst tsunami area. Maybe auntie was right to live all the way up on the volcano, Samantha thought grimly to herself. They continued up and up, gradually relaxing as they went.

As soon as they got back to Calypso's, Samantha jogged home across the street. It was past dinner time, and her parents were both home, watching the news about the incoming tsunami. It wasn't locally generated but was from an earthquake under the seafloor just off the coast of Peru.

She went into her room, dragging a bed stand into the middle of the room and putting a lit candle on it. There was no way to be sure if and how strong the tsunami would be, they said on the news. Maybe it would be stronger hitting California, maybe it would be weak when it reached California and Hawaii. But Samantha knew better. She looked at the candle and she knew better, she felt the coming menace. It had already slammed into Ecuador's Galápagos Islands with deadly effect. It was coming to kill, and she had to stop it. She began the dance around the candle, chanting to get warmed up:

"Once to divine you,
Again in adulation…"

She could feel the fire springing to life under her, within her. This was normal, a familiar feeling now. Perhaps it had always been there, she just didn't know others didn't feel the same way. Far away there was something cold and evil. When she turned, she felt cold coming from that side, from the southeast. It wouldn't be so worrisome if it was from Japan, since they were on the east side of the island, or downwind if you will from something coming from the west. Stuff that comes from the west, hits the west side of the island. Stuff that comes from the east, hits the east side of the island. When she turned, the side of her facing southeast felt a chill, not exactly from the air, but deep inside. As she turned, the chill was constant.

She could hear the news in the other room, but it was all the way from Hilo. It wasn't going to hit Hilo, Hilo was protected by a point. It was going to hit here, and she knew it. Her phone started ringing; it was grandma.

"You get to dancing, this is it," grandma said. "You have to fight water with fire."

Samantha explained what she was doing to her grandmother.

"Don't do it in the house! You'll burn the place down! Get out in a field like I taught you, don't go getting Miranda killed like foolish Evangelique. Don't stop the dance til you feel the cold retreat."

Samantha knew what she meant, but she wasn't sure what she could do. Sure, she could influence the weather some, but the earthquake had happened. She could hear the news reports. Mazatlan was all but destroyed, the lower parts of the town washed out to sea.

She called Kyle, who came out with Calypso to help her build a fire. She wasn't sure it would help but why not? She started with her candle, dancing around it while they built layers of paper, kindling, and wood around it. They had to keep relighting the candle as it kept getting blown out, and it was feeling colder and colder, she felt like it might even snuff out the warmth within her. What did that mean? They would all die? What if the tsunami caused a massive underground landslide? Forget about the lower portions of Mazatlan, if the Hilina Slump went all at once, Hawaii and the West Coast of North and South America would be history. There were too many people for an evacuation to be possible; you couldn't evacuate all of Los Angeles, the city of angels. Millions would be killed in under 24 hours.

"Get it lit," she urged Kyle. He complied, and it lit well. He was no stranger to barbecuing on the beach, and the breeze wasn't going to stop him from getting a decent fire going.

"More wood," she said, spinning and feeling her fingers hot and happy again, full of energy as she started the evocation. By the time he was back with some logs from their garage, the fire was bright, the wood was gone, and there was just a glowing pit of coals, looking as though it was burning lower into the ground, like a fire made on snow gradually sinking.

Kyle threw the wood into the newly formed pit, as Calypso

reported the first waves were beginning to arrive. Samantha was feeling warmer, that was for sure, but grandma's words rang true, she needed to do the invocation.

"The waves have started arriving," Calypso said in a panic. "Kyle they're big, the outrigger storage hut is getting destroyed!"

"What!?!?" Kyle exclaimed, jumping up to check out the video feed on Cal's smartphone.

Samantha was terrified. They were far enough up the volcano to withstand any normal tsunami. Tsunamis were usually only 10-50 feet. But the Hilina Slump could release a tsunami 1000 feet tall, maybe bigger. They'd be killed. Hilo would be gone. Tahiti would have to send a new priestess to protect the north Pacific.

For the first time since this began, she glanced up at the volcano rather than at the sea. It stood stalwart, resolute, warm underneath. No tsunami would destroy the volcano, rooted into the depths of the Earth. She looked at her fingers, only possessed with a light glow so far. She slapped her hands together, and the ground shook beneath their feet. Kilauea heard her call.

She shook her head. No fear of lahar would stop her. She smacked her hands together as violently, as hard as she could, and the ground roared under their feet, shaking so violently it didn't stop for about five seconds, as she began the invocation:

"Under the Earth, hot as Hades
My blood the magma boils
A vessel to hold my heat
Another mountain but oh so small
From within to without to within
My blood the magma boils
Not heat will burn
No fire will char
No lava will desecrate
Only will it consecrate
Burning away the useless
Clearing away the evil"

The ground under her was glowing red, and she saw rubber melting off the shoes on her feet. She kicked them off to the side, where they continued burning.

Kyle was watching her step through the coals, mouth agape.

"I'm good, back away plenty so you don't get burned, OK?" Samantha called to them.

Calypso grinned back and started dragging Kyle away.

The light was really coming from her fingertips now, and she could really feel the warmth, more than ever before. Around the fire she went, around it she went again. The cold was abating, but it was still coming, she felt she could feel the waves coming in, big and cold and destructive.

"The hotel on the point is gone!" Calypso announced. That was bad. That was where Miranda worked.

"Maybe they can rebuild," Calypso said optimistically. If any of us are left, Samantha thought to herself.

The coals were no longer sinking, as she chanted the invocation again, the coals started bulging up, first just to ground level, then an inch higher.

"Yes!" Samantha shouted. "Yes, come up!" She grabbed some coals and flung them in the direction of the ocean. "Come up!!!" she screamed, clapping her hands, each clap violently shaking the ground around them. Kyle and Calypso were knocked to the ground, it shook up and down so much. It looked to them that Samantha was standing on a bulging mound of lava, almost floating above the surface of the ground.

She threw more coals, realizing it was now actually lava she's summoned, in the direction of the sea. Looking down, she clapped her hands again and repeated the invocation, and the Earth shook, but this time it was like she'd uncorked a wine bottle of lava. It started to flow from under her, slowly for a moment, but then as she clapped again the speed increased, a gushing river of joy speeding out to stop the evil of the tsunami. She didn't feel any more of the cold, now. It was out there, she could feel the waves, but somehow she knew they would retreat. She was Pele, she was the volcano Kilauea, and no tsunami would touch her. She clapped her hands yet again, and saw that this wasn't the only fissure producing lava, with each clap of her hands another opened, the red glow of light illuminating the forest in each case, and sending huge amounts of smoke and dust up into the sky.

"No lahar here!" Samantha yelled rhetorically. She wouldn't be destroyed like her aunt, this was second nature, the volcano had been inside her all along.

Massive plumes of steam were coming uphill through the forest.

"The lava's in the ocean!" Calypso yelled. "You have a river of lava flowing into the ocean!"

Samantha knew she was supposed to be afraid of the lava, but it would protect the island. She clapped her hands a few more times and continued the dance. As the lava continued to flow, she felt the waves taper off. Finally she stopped. Looking down, she was standing in lava, squishy like mud between her toes. Her fingers were hard to look at they glowed so bright, with sparks coming off like arc welders whenever she moved her fingers. She grabbed some lava and hurled it at the ocean, feeling victorious. Her arms glowed red.

"The waves are gone," Calypso proclaimed. She stepped out of the lava.

"Great job Samantha!" Kyle exclaimed, coming over to give her a victory embrace. Fortunately Calypso stopped him, reminding him Samantha was probably 2000°, as hot as the lava she just stepped out of.

Relieved, Samantha plopped down beside them, the ground heating up under her glowing red. The surfcam on the hill told the story. Their pier was mostly destroyed, and a bunch of houses and hotels right on the water had taken a beating, but everything over ten feet up was fine. Most everything on the coastline was fine. Samantha had some training to do, she needed to train people to protect the Galápagos.

Back at home her mother was all anxious, saying grandma had been freaking out and calling for updates every ten minutes and was happy to hear Samantha was out dancing in the field, flinging lava about like a fire elemental. Miranda had fear in her eyes, looking over her glowing child, her baby, amazed Samantha was finally able to successfully marshal the forces that killed Miranda's elder sister.

Grandma later spoke to Samantha, explaining that she'd replaced the void of high priestesses in Hawai'i, that by virtue of her having opened large fissures and created a large lava flow, they wouldn't have to worry a lot about storms and tsunamis until Samantha grew old or sick.

That turned out to be true, for the most part, if only for Hawai'i.

Printed in Great Britain
by Amazon.co.uk, Ltd.,
Marston Gate.